MAGGIE

A GIRL OF THE STREETS

Chandler Facsimile Editions in
AMERICAN LITERATURE
Hamlin Hill, *Editor*

 Science Research Associates, Inc., 259 East Erie Street, Chicago, Illinois 60611
A Subsidiary of IBM   Distributors

MAGGIE

A GIRL OF THE STREETS

(A Story of New York)

by

STEPHEN CRANE

A FACSIMILE OF THE FIRST EDITION

With an introduction, a note on the text, and
a bibliography prepared by

DONALD PIZER
TULANE UNIVERSITY

CHANDLER PUBLISHING COMPANY

124 Spear Street, San Francisco, California 94105

CONTENTS

Maggie: A Girl of the Streets

245159

INTRODUCTION

Stephen Crane was born on November 1, 1871, in Newark, and died of tuberculosis on June 5, 1900, in Badenweiler, Germany. His best work was done principally between 1893 and 1897. It is thus tempting to portray Crane as an American Keats, as a writer whose genius flared briefly but gloriously, who crowded into a short life the pains and pleasures of several lifetimes, and whose creative work has left an indelible mark on our sensibilities. He was not a Keats, of course; even his finest work lacks the depth and finish of Keats' major poems. But there will always be attached to Crane the same sense of wonder that we accord the sudden flowering and early death of a major talent. And we will always read his best work with the same intensity that we bring to the appreciation of any object which is both aesthetically remarkable and rare.

I

Maggie: A Girl of the Streets, Crane's first extended and important work, was published in March, 1893, when he was twenty-one. How Crane came to the stylized irony of this short novel of the Bowery slums is still a mystery, though recent intensive studies of his biography and of his literary and social milieu are beginning to suggest possible approaches to a solution. Crane's father was a Methodist clergyman, his mother the daughter of prominent Methodists and herself a writer for religious periodicals. After the death of his father, Crane spent the formative years of his adolescence, from 1883 to 1888, at Asbury Park, an upper-middle-class New Jersey shore resort. There, as Edwin Cady has suggested,[1] he was educated in the relationship between voiced pieties and the eagerly seized "amusements" of a summer resort. There he encountered both the middle-class proprieties and moral uplift of the nearby Methodist and educational groups at Ocean Grove and Avon-by-the-Sea and the free life of the semiunderworld that services and frequents a resort area. There, in other words, he experienced the distinction between what men believe about themselves and what they truly are, and there he was introduced to the relationship between behavior and class. In short, he there began to absorb those awarenesses which are among the principal sources of an ironic vision of life.

Crane was thus no doubt precociously worldly when he attended Claverack College (near Hudson, New

---

[1] Cady, *Stephen Crane* (New York, 1962), pp. 24–25.

York) between 1888 and 1890 and when he began to help his brother Townley report shore news for the *New York Tribune* during the summers of those years. His personal and moral independence seems to have flowered into a way of life by the time he entered Lafayette College in the fall of 1890. It also characterized his career at Syracuse University, to which he transferred in midyear. At both schools he ignored the institutional for that which satisfied his own interests; in other words, he ignored his courses in favor of sports and reading. At Syracuse, he became the local correspondent for the *New York Tribune*, visiting the police courts for the sensational items which constituted the staple for "upstate" columns in the New York papers. And there he began to write a story about a prostitute.

The outlines of Crane's temperament as it developed in his later career are visible by the time he left Syracuse (and all formal education) in the spring of 1891. Daniel Hoffman has described Crane as an isolato,[2] as a man separated from his fellows and from his culture by his doubts and heresies. But Crane was also throughout his life the kind of man who played on baseball teams and joined clubs, and who cultivated and maintained lifelong friendships. Perhaps a more useful way of characterizing Crane is to see that he both shared in the culture of his time and wished to divorce himself from it,

---

[2] Hoffman, *The Poetry of Stephen Crane* (New York, 1957), p. 6.

that he attempted (to use the jargon appropriate to the 1890s) to pursue both the Strenuous Life and Bohemianism.[3] So on the one hand there is the Crane who shared the life of New York artists and medical students (1891 to 1895), the Crane who frequented Bowery dives and Tenderloin cafes and who was fascinated by "fallen" women. There is the Crane, in other words, who wished his unorthodox personal life to be his own business, and who, like the expatriates of the 1920s, finally had to escape to Europe to assure the freedom to live as he desired—in his case, to live with a woman not his wife. But on the other hand there is the Crane who loved sports and camping and horseback riding, who said he learned about war from football, the Crane of the active, vigorous life who became the writer who wished to experience the basic emotions of life in their proper context and so exposed himself to enemy fire in Cuba. This is Crane the newspaperman, first in the Bowery and Tenderloin, then in Greece and Cuba. The two modes of life coalesce in the image of the writer who is alienated from his world primarily because he wishes to seek out the concrete experiences of life on his own terms in order to recreate them in his own terms. This is ultimately the image of the writer as romantic hero as that image re-

[3] For Crane and the Strenuous Life, see particularly Cady, pp. 81–85.

ceives its first great personification in Byron and is kept alive by Crane and by Hemingway and Mailer.

During the summer of 1891 Crane again reported shore news at Asbury Park, meeting in August his first author, Hamlin Garland, who was lecturing at Avon. In the fall he began a kind of double life, moving between the New Jersey home of his brother Edmund and the New York flats of the students and aspiring artists he was coming to know. In the summer of 1892 he helped his brother Townley once more (again meeting Garland), but now also succeeded in breaking into the *Tribune* with a number of sketches based on camping experiences in New York's Sullivan County as well as one sketch of New York street life. In the fall he settled in New York, moving in with a group of young men (principally medical students) who occupied most of a boarding house on Avenue A near 57th Street on the far East Side. They called themselves the Pendennis Club. There he lived for approximately eight months, during which time he wrote and published *Maggie*.

The facts concerning the composition of *Maggie* have been obscured not only by a lack of detailed knowledge of Crane's activities during his early career but by the inaccuracies of Crane's first biographer, Thomas Beer, whose *Stephen Crane* appeared in 1923. There seems little doubt that Crane was writing a story about

a prostitute while at Syracuse in the spring of 1891,
since Frank Noxon, one of his classmates, later recalled
such a story in documents independent of Beer's account.[4] The next verifiable information about the novel
is a letter received by the Library of Congress on January 19, 1893, in which Crane inclosed a typescript
title page of a novel called "A Girl of the Streets" by
Stephen Crane and asked that the work be copyrighted.[5]
Beer posited two intermediate versions of the novel: one
written in late December of 1891, and a revision of this
version in early 1892.[6]

Beer's account of four versions of *Maggie* is based
on two errors. His belief that a second version was written just before Christmas, 1891, derived from the rec-
ollection of Crane's friend Wallis McHarg that Crane
had shown him this version (in which the book lacked
its full title and the characters were unnamed) in January, 1892. But McHarg also recalled that he had by
this time read Crane's Sullivan County sketches, which
Crane had sent him in clipping form and which (as
Beer was unaware) had appeared in July, 1892.[7] In

[4] See Noxon to Max J. Herzberg, December 7, 1926; in *Stephen
Crane: Letters,* ed. R. W. Stallman and Lillian Gilkes (New York,
1960), p. 335.

[5] *Letters,* pp. 13–14.

[6] Beer, *Stephen Crane* (New York, 1923), pp. 80–86.

[7] Beer (p. 81) believed that the sketches were set in the Wyoming
Valley of Pennsylvania, which suggests that he did not look them up
in the *Tribune* (they were uncollected at the time) and was fuzzy
about when they had been published.

late February Crane wrote McHarg that the book had been titled "Maggie: A Girl of the Streets." Thus, the entire McHarg account really belongs to the winter of 1892–93 rather than to that of 1891–92. Crane wrote a draft of *Maggie* just before Christmas, 1892, which he showed to McHarg. Continuing work on the book, he copyrighted it in January, but still under its incomplete name. By February he had named the book (or his brother William had, in Beer's account), as he wrote Mc-Harg, and was probably trying to interest editors in it.

Beer's second error was his dating of a letter by Hamlin Garland to Richard Watson Gilder, editor of the *Century,* as March 23, 1892.[8] In later years Gilder recalled his shocked reaction to *Maggie,* but he was probably remembering his response to the published volume rather than to the manuscript. For as Robert Mane has shown, the letter of March 23, which concerns a Crane manuscript that Garland was recommending to Gilder, is about *The Black Riders* and *The Red Badge of Courage,* not *Maggie* (as Beer believed), and thus must be dated 1894.[9] Since Beer used the Garland to Gilder letter to establish an early 1892 revision of *Maggie,* this aspect of his history of the novel's genesis also lacks substance.

[8] Beer, p. 86. Stallman and Gilkes date it tentatively as March 23, 1893, in *Letters,* p. 16.

[9] Mane, "Une Rencontre Littéraire: Hamlin Garland et Stephen Crane," *Etudes Anglaises,* XVII (January–March, 1964), 34.

So Beer's story of the composition of *Maggie,* an account accepted by all of Crane's biographers and critics, is mistaken and must be replaced.[10] It is probable that Crane did draft a story about a prostitute while at Syracuse, but what kind of story it was we do not know. It may bear very little relationship to *Maggie.* And it was probably not an extensive or finished work, or he undoubtedly would have mentioned it to Hamlin Garland in the summers of 1891 and 1892. Crane's work before the fall of 1892 is best represented not by an incipient *Maggie* but by his Sullivan County sketches, which displayed what he later called his "clever, Rudyard-Kip-

[10] Another misleading account of the history of *Maggie* which must also now be discarded is that by Willis F. Johnson, "The Launching of Stephen Crane," *Literary Digest International Book Review,* IV (April, 1926), 288–90. Johnson, writing some thirty-five years after the events of the early 1890s, and basing his account partially on Beer, is almost totally inaccurate in his dating. For example, he places Crane at Syracuse in the fall of 1890 rather than in the spring of 1891, and he dates the publication of the Sullivan County sketches as the summer of 1891 rather than the summer of 1892. Johnson claimed that Crane showed him the manuscript of *Maggie* at Asbury Park in the summer of 1891 shortly after showing him two of his Sullivan County sketches. Johnson also recalled that Crane agreed at this time that it would be advisable to publish the book pseudonymously. Since Crane almost certainly did not reach this decision until early 1893, it seems probable that Johnson, who was day editor of the *New York Tribune,* was one of the editors to whom Crane brought the manuscript of *Maggie* in early 1893. In recollecting this event, however, Johnson confused the incident with the occasion when Crane brought him two of the Sullivan County sketches (which Crane actually did, though in 1892, not 1891) and therefore placed both events in the summer of 1891 at Asbury Park.

ling style" of comic hyperbole and anticlimax both in language and in situation.

But during 1891–92 Crane was also moving toward *Maggie* in two ways: he was becoming fascinated by Bowery life, with its poverty and violence yet its profound social and moral implications; and he was becoming aware that there were writers in America who were committed to a truthful portrayal of their impressions of all ranges of life whatever the proprieties of that portrayal. The impact of the Bowery on Crane can be dated from the fall of 1891 when he began to spend much time in New York and when he told Helen Trent that it was "the only interesting place" in the city.[11] Crane's introduction to "advanced" literary ideas probably dates from his meeting with Garland in the summer of 1891 and from his reporting Garland's lecture at Avon on the ideas and fiction of William Dean Howells. Howells, Garland said and Crane reported, "does not insist upon any special material, but only that the novelist be true to himself and to things as he sees them."[12] In later years Crane echoed this theory of art several times, and associated his acceptance of it with the ideas of Howells and Garland and with the

[11] Beer, p. 61.

[12] [Stephen Crane], "Howells Discussed at Avon-by-the-Sea," *New York Tribune*, August 18, 1891, p. 5. Republished in *The New York City Sketches of Stephen Crane*, ed. R. W. Stallman and E. R. Hagemann (New York, 1966), p. 267.

year 1892. So he could write in 1896 that "I had no other purpose in writing 'Maggie' than to show people to people as they seem to me. If that be evil, make the most of it." [13] Earlier that year he had stated this idea even more directly: "I understand that a man is born into the world with his own pair of eyes, and he is not at all responsible for his vision—he is merely responsible for his quality of personal honesty." [14] It was to this creed, then, that Crane obliquely referred when in a letter of early 1894 he wrote that he had renounced in the fall of 1892 "the clever school in literature," [15] and it was to this creed that he directly referred when in 1895 he inscribed a copy of *The Red Badge* to Howells as a token of the "veneration and gratitude of Stephen Crane for many things he has learned of the common man and, above all, for a certain re-adjustment of his point of view victoriously concluded some time in 1892." [16]

The theory of the composition of *Maggie* which I have been sketching thus accepts literally Crane's remark to Lily Brandon Munroe in early April, 1893, that he had worked hard for three months because "I wrote a book." [17] Crane, I believe, is alluding not to a revi-

---

[13] Crane to Catherine Harris, November 12, 1896; *Letters*, p. 133.
[14] Crane to John N. Hilliard, January, 1896; *Letters*, p. 110.
[15] Crane to Lily Brandon Munroe, March, 1894; *Letters*, p. 31.
[16] *Letters*, p. 62.
[17] Crane to Lily Brandon Munroe, April, 1893; *Letters*, p. 20.

sion of his 1891 story about a prostitute but to an initial full composition and revision of *Maggie,* a task undertaken in the spirit of his decision to turn from clever to serious writing. *Maggie* is a work of the imagination. But it is also a self-conscious work in the sense that it stems from its author's conscious involvement in a particular milieu and from his acceptance of critical ideas which encouraged him to deal with that milieu in his own terms, to portray it with "his own eyes."

After completing *Maggie* in late February or early March, 1893, Crane apparently attempted to publish the work commercially. Soon despairing of this possibility, he borrowed some money from his brother William, a successful lawyer, and had the book privately printed. The paper-covered book called *Maggie: A Girl of the Streets,* which was printed in late March, 1893, has a number of curious characteristics. As Howells noted in 1895, one could not claim that it was "published," [18] since it was offered for sale at only one bookstore and received only one review. Moreover, the volume contained many typographical errors (principally misspellings) and was issued pseudonymously, by one Johnston Smith. Lastly, no printer or publisher was indicated anywhere in the volume.

[18] W. D. Howells, "Life and Letters," *Harper's Weekly,* XXXIX (June 8, 1895), 533.

An explanation of the many errors in the text lies obviously in the fact that Crane was not given an opportunity to read proof, which suggests as well that very little time elapsed between his decision to publish the novel himself and its appearance. The reasons for the pseudonym of the author and anonymity of the printer are more problematical. Beer attributed to Crane the desire to startle the world by identifying himself once the book was acclaimed. Crane, however, acknowledged his authorship from the outset by sending inscribed copies to various friends and by allowing Garland to review the book in June, 1893, as by Crane.[19] Both the pseudonym and the printer's reluctance to be identified probably stem from the same source—a fear that the book might be considered pornographic. Crane himself had no such conception of the work; but he may have wished to obscure at least partially the connection between the book and his prominent Methodist family, just as the firm of medical and religious publishers which printed the work did not wish to acknowledge a connection with it. After all, the central figure in the novel was a Bowery "girl of the streets," and the book was thickly garnished with profanity.

To Crane's disappointment, the work received no at-

[19] See *Letters,* pp. 14–15, and Garland's "An Ambitious French Novel and a Modest American Story," *Arena,* VIII (June, 1893), xi–xii.

tention (except for Garland's brief review) either as pornography or as art. However, it did allow him to renew his friendship with Garland and to meet Howells (through Garland), who praised the book and encouraged the young author. And so Crane was launched as a novelist. Still very much the garret artist, he had nevertheless written and published a book in which he had faith and in which those whom he respected had faith. Soon after the appearance of *Maggie* he began to write *The Red Badge of Courage*.

II

To describe the origins of *Maggie* entirely in terms of the events of Crane's early career is to ignore another important matrix of the novel—the Bowery slums as reality and as cultural image. The Bowery itself is a slightly curving north-south street about one mile long. It extends from just below Canal Street to 4th Street, almost in the center of lower Manhattan. Its name derives from the Dutch word for farm, and the street was originally "the road to the farm," that is, to Governor Stuyvesant's farm. During the early nineteenth century the Bowery was a prominent commercial street. But with the impact of mass immigration on lower Manhattan, beginning about midcentury, and with the movement uptown of both the theater section and the better residential areas, the street began to degenerate. By the late nineteenth century the Bowery was lined with beerhalls and saloons, with cheap lodging houses and restaurants, and with missions. Its surrounding neighborhoods were tenement slums with distinct ethnic divisions. South of Canal were the Irish; north of Canal and east of the Bowery were the Germans; and north of Canal and west of the Bowery were the Italians. During the 1880s and 1890s Jews had begun to replace the Germans, and the Italians had begun to move north into Greenwich Village.

Crane's Bowery slum is essentially that of its oldest and worse tenement section, below Canal, and consists primarily of Irish with a sprinkling of Germans and English. This ethnic setting is clearer in *George's Mother,* which was written in 1894 and which is set in the same tenement as *Maggie,* than it is in the earlier novel. George Kelcey's world contains a Zeusentell and a Jones, but it is populated for the most part by O'Connors, Corcorans, Connigans, and Callahans. Crane alludes to the nearby Jewish and Italian neighborhoods occasionally in each of the novels. In *Maggie,* for example, he introduces what appears to be a Jewish-German sweatshop owner, and in *George's Mother* he refers to a street fight between an Italian and an Irishman. His portrait of the Bowery thus accurately reflects its ethnic frontiers.

Maggie's tenement is near the East River, in the

area which is at present an immense public-housing district between the Brooklyn and Manhattan bridges. But Crane was writing the book in a room overlooking the East River near 57th Street, and so on page 5 he describes the convicts in the city prison on Blackwell's Island (now Welfare Island) who were visible from his window. In general, however, his Bowery detail is accurate. Rum Alley and Devil's Row are invented street names but may have had their actual counterparts, just as the "great green-hued hall" of page 56 is the Atlantic Garden on the Bowery.[20]

Crane's Bowery dialect is achieved primarily by the almost complete disappearance of the "th" sound, by the omission of many final consonants, by the slurring of a number of vowels, and by much bad grammar and profanity—particularly *hell, damn,* and *Gawd.* Both Garland and Howells admired the dialect and thought it authentic. Garland called it "crisp, direct, terse," and Howells praised it as "the best tough dialect which has yet found its way into print." [21] Some of its excesses can perhaps be attributed to the tendency in Crane's day to use dialect in local-color fiction as an aesthetic crutch, as a way of achieving verisimilitude by literalism. But to Crane the dialect and profanity were matters

[20] See R. W. Stallman, "Crane's *Maggie:* A Reassessment," *The Houses That James Built* (East Lansing, Mich., 1961), p. 75.
[21] Garland, "An Ambitious French Novel . . . ," p. xii; and Howells, "Life and Letters," p. 533.

of truth-telling. " 'That is the way they *talk,*' " he explained to Howells.[22]

Crane's depiction of the Bowery slums reveals not only the impact of the Bowery as actuality but of the Bowery and the slums as a complex cultural image. One strain in this image was that established by Zola in *L'Assommoir,* in which the poverty, alcoholism, and sexuality of Parisian slum life are depicted as uncontrollable destructive forces. Another is the image of the slums created by such social moralists as Jacob Riis, author of *How the Other Half Lives* (1891), and B. O. Flower, editor of the *Arena.* Their work emphasizes both the concrete evils of slum conditions and the need to correct these conditions. A final strain is that which combines the sensational novel of seduction of the poor working girl with the religious tract warning of the pleasures of the city into a conception that man's moral strength and God's grace are the only bulwarks against the evils of modern city life. Early critics of Crane's work were prone to stress the influence of French naturalism on *Maggie;* more recently, Crane's family and religious background and the heavy flow of American tract and social-reform writing on the slums have been seen as major influences. No doubt all played their role in helping shape the creation of *Maggie,* though it is

[22] W. D. Howells "Frank Norris," *North American Review,* CLXXV (December, 1902), 770.

difficult to separate the threads of influence. Crane's plot of the seduction, the fall into prostitution, and the early death of a girl of the slums is archetypal in the cultural imagination of the 1890s, as are the alcoholism, the violence, and the mission religion of the slums as a setting. This is the "plot" and "setting" of the slum as imaginative reality, whether that reality appears in Zola, in social criticism, or in fictional and religious moralism. What is distinctive in *Maggie* is therefore not its subject matter but its style—that is to say, its irony, an irony so pervasive that within it lies both the theme and the form of the work.

III

One way of approaching the distinctiveness of *Maggie* as a novel of the slums is to compare two relevant statements about environment and morality. The first, by Arthur D. Vinton, appeared in the *Arena* in April, 1891:

Take, for example, a boy brought up in the slums around Tompkins Square, in New York City. From his earliest childhood he is of necessity familiar with all manner of wickedness; the best dressed women of his neighborhood are fallen women; the boys who have the most money to spend are those who lead vicious lives; the brightest house is the saloon. New York City is the metropolis of vice as she is of trade, and every vice in the long catalogue of sin has a representative practitioner among the varied nationalities that swarm her slums. . . . Can a child spend his life amid such environment without being, both in body and brain, affected by it? For a child to grow up virtuous in such a locality is little less than a miracle—and the day of miracles has passed.

If a child is born and bred to manhood in such environment, he has no choice but to become wicked. He is not free to choose good from evil. He has no discriminating sense of right and wrong. His moral responsibility is *nil*.[23]

The second statement, by Crane, is one which he inscribed in a number of copies of *Maggie* which he sent to friends in March, 1893:

It is inevitable that you will be greatly shocked by this book but continue please with all possible courage to the end. For it tries to show that environment is a tremendous thing in the world and frequently shapes lives regardless. If one proves that theory one makes room in Heaven for all sorts of souls (notably an occasional street girl) who are not confidently expected to be there by many excellent people.[24]

The primary difference between the two statements is not that of theme. Both writers accept an environmental determinism which frees the slum dweller from moral responsibility. The difference is rather that of ethical

---

[23] Arthur D. Vinton, "Morality and Environment," *Arena,* III (April, 1891), 574. Quoted by Lars Ahnebrink, *The Beginnings of Naturalism in American Fiction* (Cambridge, Mass., 1950), p. 79.
[24] *Letters,* p. 14.

thrust or direction. Vinton's rhetoric—his emphasis on the child and on the absolute power of slum conditions —seeks to move us to change these conditions, to provide environments in which moral choice is a possibility rather than a miracle. Crane's strategy, on the other hand, is to engage us to question our moral assumptions. He does not so much wish us to contribute to Settlement Houses as to ask ourselves—as excellent people— whether we do not tacitly judge others by their circumstances rather than by either their essential nature (Maggie *is* a "miracle" of slum virtue) or by their responsibility for their circumstances.

Both writers are addressing a middle-class audience. But whereas Vinton appeals to the conscience of his audience, Crane wishes to shock his readers into recognizing that most moral judgments have little to do with reality. Crane's method of achieving this effect in the novel itself is not that of explicit statement. Rather, he uses the ironic technique of having his slum characters adopt middle-class moral poses and attitudes which are totally inapplicable to the truths of their lives. The world of the slum is an amoral jungle of physical, economic, and sexual struggle, but its inhabitants constantly cast themselves in moral and romantic roles absorbed from the missions and from popular melodrama. From Jimmie fighting squalidly for the "honor" of Rum Alley, to Pete's concern for the "respectability" of his saloon, to the supreme irony of Mary "fergiving" her errant daughter, the novel is poised on the ironic relationship between moral positions and the human inadequacies disguised or compensated for by these positions. It is no wonder that the novel is permeated with a sense of the theatrical, a sense of role-playing in which, like Maggie at the Bowery melodrama, the principal characters identify themselves with moral and romantic roles—a Knight, a Rescued Maiden, a Vengeful Brother, a Christian Mother—and play out these roles before an admiring audience. It is as though Crane were seeking to demonstrate that the world at large is a theater of moral roles. One of the appeals of the Bowery to Crane is that the crudity of its moral melodrama makes vividly explicit this universal role-playing.

What I have been suggesting, in other words, is that just as the theme of *The Red Badge of Courage* is not war but rather man's attempt to know himself, so *Maggie* is not primarily about life in the slums but is rather about the relationship of self-satisfying moral and romantic roles to the actualities of experience. It is this pervasive ironic vision of moral reality which lends *Maggie* its peculiar force as a novel. Indeed, in this sense *Maggie* is more coherent than Crane's other major works (with the exception of "The Open Boat"), for Crane's irony can also shade off into authorial ambivalence toward his major characters, as in *The Red Badge*.

Crane's *Maggie* is in the fictional mode pioneered by Mark Twain in *Adventures of Huckleberry Finn.* As in *Huck Finn,* Crane's ironic portrayal of the vision and beliefs of lower-class characters serves principally to satirize middle-class life. *Maggie* and *Huck Finn* suggest that some modification is required of Erich Auerbach's concept (in his *Mimesis*) that the serious treatment of lower-class life in the late nineteenth century reveals primarily the greater significance and worth attributed to that life by both the author and his society. It appears clear from these works by Twain and Crane that in America at least the subject matter of the lower classes was often less an intrinsic interest than a device by which to satirize the values of the middle-class world which still constituted the primary audience for any literature beyond the meretricious. One suspects that the recent "kitchen sink" school of drama in England has used its lower-class setting in much the same way.

Crane is not only an ironist but also a symbolist. Maggie's lambrequin can serve as an example of a naturalistic symbol as used by Crane. Drawn from the commonplace realities of lower-class life, its purpose is to communicate what is inarticulate and unconscious in Maggie, her sense that beauty is associated with love and that beauty must therefore be made visible if love is to be known. The technique is that of suggesting through symbols which are both stylized and gross the most profound and the most intense human concerns. The contribution of the naturalistic symbol to fiction is parallel to the contribution made to poetry by the imagery of Whitman; the symbol makes possible the oblique representation of the deepest nature of man by means of the often grotesquely common realities of his daily life. This is the method of Joyce and Faulkner, and is a technique inseparable from much of modern fiction.

In a sense, then, *Maggie* stands at a half-way point in the road that leads from the Civil War to the modern American literary imagination. For on the one hand— as Frank Norris noted—Crane stands aside from his lower-class world in his roles as ironist and satirist; [25] but on the other, his naturalistic symbolism—the lambrequin or Jimmie's relationship to his wagon—suggests an involvement in the possible depths of his lower-class characters which is at odds with his ironic stance. Perhaps one can say that *Maggie* represents a Crane certain of his fictional voice but not yet entirely certain of his feelings, and that some of the unresolved complexities in our response to the work arise from its transitional character both in the history of American literature since the Civil War and within Crane's ca-

[25] Frank Norris, "Stephen Crane's Stories of Life in the Slums," [San Francisco] *Wave*, XV (July 4, 1896), 13. Republished in *The Literary Criticism of Frank Norris*, ed. Donald Pizer (Austin, Texas, 1964), p. 166.

reer. But such transitional works are often the most compelling and rewarding, and it is on this basis—if no other—that *Maggie* increasingly attracts our attention as we learn more about Crane and as we seek to learn more about the 1890s.

ACKNOWLEDGMENTS

I wish to thank Mr. William H. Runge of the Alderman Library, University of Virginia, for his unfailing courtesy and for his aid in making available a microfilm copy of the 1893 *Maggie*. Professor Max Westbrook, of the University of Texas, was kind enough to read my Introduction and to make helpful suggestions.

A NOTE ON THE TEXT

The present edition of *Maggie* is a facsimile of the copy of the 1893 edition in the Tracy W. McGregor Library of the Alderman Library, University of Virginia. Early in 1896 Crane undertook to revise *Maggie* for publication by D. Appleton and Company, which had published *The Red Badge of Courage* in 1895. His revision consisted of correcting typographical errors (some eighty-nine, according to Maurice Bassan [26]); removing or softening a great deal of the profanity; and making many minor verbal changes. His only revision of any length was to omit Maggie's encounter with the "huge fat man in torn and greasy garments" at the close of Chapter XVII. The 1896 revision of *Maggie* served as the text for all subsequent editions of the novel (including the collected edition of 1925–26) [27] until very recently, when both a facsimile edi-

[26] Maurice Bassan, *Stephen Crane's "Maggie": Text and Context* (Belmont, Calif., 1966), p. xv.

[27] The collected-edition version of *Maggie* also incorporated some of the minor variations present in the 1896 English edition of the novel.

tion and a partially edited version of the 1893 publication have appeared.

The primary justifications for a reasonably priced facsimile edition of the 1893 edition are, first, the rarity of the book (it is one of the most costly items in the American rare-book market) and, second, its closeness to the verbal style of the Crane of 1892–93, a style untouched by editorial restrictions or conventions. Crane's correspondence with Ripley Hitchcock, his Appleton editor, leaves little doubt that Crane was cutting a good deal of the profanity in order to make the book acceptable to a respectable publisher. He also gave Hitchcock permission to make additional changes in the text as Hitchcock saw fit.[28] In all, the 1893 *Maggie* represents the younger Crane—strongly flavored, occasionally smart-alecky—and deserves to be more readily available and more widely known.

[28] See *Letters,* pp. 112–14, 118–19, 122.

A SELECTIVE BIBLIOGRAPHY

PRINCIPAL EDITIONS OF *MAGGIE*

Smith, Johnston. *Maggie: A Girl of the Streets.* [New York, 1893].

Crane, Stephen. *Maggie: A Girl of the Streets.* Appleton, New York, 1896.

Crane, Stephen. *Maggie: A Child of the Streets.* Heinemann, London, 1896.

Follett, Wilson, ed. *Major Conflicts,* Vol. X of *The Work of Stephen Crane.* Knopf, New York, 1926.

Stallman, R. W., ed. *Stephen Crane: An Omnibus.* Knopf, New York, 1952.

Gibson, William M., ed. *The Red Badge of Courage and Selected Prose and Poetry.* Rinehart, New York, 1956.

Bassan, Maurice, ed. *Stephen Crane's "Maggie": Text and Context.* Wadsworth, Belmont, Calif., 1966.

Katz, Joseph, ed. *Maggie: A Girl of the Streets.* Scholars' Facsimiles and Reprints, Gainesville, Florida, 1966.

BIOGRAPHICAL AND CRITICAL STUDIES

BOOKS:

Ahnebrink, Lars. *The Beginnings of Naturalism in American Fiction.* Cambridge, Mass., 1950.

Beer, Thomas. *Stephen Crane.* New York, 1923.

Berryman, John. *Stephen Crane.* New York, 1950.

Cady, Edwin H. *Stephen Crane.* New York, 1962.

Hoffman, Daniel. *The Poetry of Stephen Crane.* New York, 1957.

Linson, Corwin K. *My Stephen Crane,* ed. Edwin H. Cady. Syracuse, 1958.

Pizer, Donald. *Realism and Naturalism in Nineteenth-Century American Literature.* Carbondale, Ill., 1966.

Stallman, R. W. *The Houses That James Built.* East Lansing, Mich., 1961.

Stallman, R. W., and Lillian Gilkes. *Stephen Crane: Letters.* New York, 1960.

Walcutt, Charles C. *American Literary Naturalism, A Divided Stream.* Minneapolis, 1956.

Ziff, Larzer. *The American 1890s.* New York, 1966.

ARTICLES BEARING SIGNIFICANTLY ON *Maggie:*

Brennan, Joseph X. "Ironic and Symbolic Structure in Crane's *Maggie," Nineteenth-Century Fiction,* XVI (March, 1962), 303–15.

Colvert, James B. "Structure and Theme in Stephen Crane's Fiction," *Modern Fiction Studies,* V (Autumn, 1959), 199–208.

Cunliffe, Marcus. "Stephen Crane and the American Background of *Maggie,*" *American Quarterly,* VII (Spring, 1955), 31–44.

Fitelson, David. "Stephen Crane's *Maggie* and Darwinism," *American Quarterly,* XVI (Summer, 1964), 182–94.

Gullason, Thomas A. "The Sources of Stephen Crane's *Maggie,*" *Philological Quarterly,* XXXVIII (October, 1959), 497–502.

Gullason, Thomas A. "Thematic Patterns in Stephen Crane's Early Novels," *Nineteenth-Century Fiction,* XVI (June, 1961), 59–67.

Katz, Joseph. "The *Maggie* Nobody Knows," *Modern Fiction Studies,* XII (Summer, 1966), 200–212.

Mane, Robert. "Une Rencontre Littéraire : Hamlin Garland et Stephen Crane," *Études Anglaises,* XVII (January–March, 1964), 30–46.

Overmyer, Janet. "The Structure of Crane's *Maggie,*" *University of Kansas City Review,* XXIX (Autumn, 1962), 71–72.

Stallman, R. W. "Stephen Crane's Revision of *Maggie: A Girl of the Streets,*" *American Literature,* XXVI (January, 1955), 528–36.

Stein, William B. "New Testament Inversions in Crane's *Maggie,*" *Modern Language Notes,* LXXIII (April, 1958), 268–72.

West, Ray B., Jr. "Stephen Crane : Author in Transition," *American Literature,* XXXIV (May, 1962), 215–28.

Westbrook, Max. "Stephen Crane's Social Ethic," *American Quarterly,* XIV (Winter, 1962), 587–96.

The Facsimile of

MAGGIE: A GIRL OF THE STREETS

MAGGIE

A Girl of the Streets

(A STORY OF NEW YORK)

By

JOHNSTON SMITH

Copyrighted

MAGGIE

A

GIRL OF THE STREETS

(A STORY OF NEW YORK)

BY

JOHNSTON SMITH

A GIRL OF THE STREETS:

A STORY OF NEW YORK.

———

CHAPTER I.

A very little boy stood upon a heap of gravel for the honor of Rum Alley. He was throwing stones at howling urchins from Devil's Row who were circling madly about the heap and pelting at him.

His infantile countenance was livid with fury. His small body was writhing in the delivery of great, crimson oaths.

"Run, Jimmie, run! Dey'll get yehs," screamed a retreating Rum Alley child.

"Naw," responded Jimmie with a valiant roar, "dese micks can't make me run."

Howls of renewed wrath went up from Devil's Row throats. Tattered gamins on the right made a furious assault on the gravel heap. On their small, convulsed faces there shone the grins of true assassins. As they charged, they threw stones and cursed in shrill chorus.

The little champion of Rum Alley stumbled precipitately down the other side. His coat had been torn to shreds in a scuffle, and his hat was gone. He had bruises on twenty parts of his body, and blood was dripping from a cut in his head. His wan features wore a look of a tiny, insane demon.

On the ground, children from Devil's Row closed in on their antagonist. He crooked his left arm defensively about his head and fought with cursing fury. The little boys ran to and fro, dodging, hurling stones and swearing in barbaric trebles.

From a window of an apartment house that upreared its form from amid squat, ignorant stables, there leaned a curious woman. Some laborers, unloading a scow at a dock at the river, paused for a moment and regarded the fight. The engineer of a passive tugboat hung lazily to a railing and watched. Over on the Island, a worm of yellow convicts came from the shadow of a grey ominous building and crawled slowly along the river's bank.

A stone had smashed into Jimmie's mouth. Blood was bubbling over his chin and down upon his ragged shirt. Tears made furrows on his dirt-stained cheeks. His thin legs had begun to tremble and turn weak, causing his small body to reel. His roaring curses of the first part of the fight had changed to a blasphemous chatter.

In the yells of the whirling mob of Devil's Row children there were notes of joy like songs of triumphant savagery. The little boys seemed to leer gloatingly at the blood upon the other child's face.

Down the avenue came boastfully sauntering a lad of sixteen years, although the chronic sneer of an ideal manood already sat upon his lips. His hat was tipped with an air of challenge over his eye. Between his teeth, a cigar stump was tilted at the angle of defiance. He walked with a certain swing of the shoulders which appalled the timid. He glanced over into the vacant lot in which the little raving boys from Devil's Row seethed about the shrieking and tearful child from Rum Alley.

"Gee!" he murmured with interest, "A scrap. Gee!"

He strode over to the cursing circle, swinging his shoulders in a manner which denoted that he held victory in his fists. He approached at the back of one of the most deeply engaged of the Devil's Row children.

"Ah, what deh hell," he said, and smote the deeply-engaged one on the back of the head. The little boy fell to the ground and gave a hoarse, tremendous howl. He scrambled to his feet,

and perceiving, evidently, the size of his assail-
ant, ran quickly off, shouting alarms.   The
entire Devil's Row party followed him.   They
came to a stand a short distance away and
yelled taunting oaths at the boy with the
chronic sneer.   The latter, momentarily, paid
no attention to them.

"What deh hell, Jimmie?" he asked of the
small champion.

Jimmie wiped his blood-wet features with
his sleeve.

"Well, it was dis way, Pete, see! I was
goin' teh lick dat Riley kid and dey all pitched
on me."

Some Rum Alley children now came foward.
The party stood for a moment exchanging
vainglorious remarks with Devil's Row.   A
few stones were thrown at long distances,
and words of challenge passed between small
warriors.   Then the Rum Alley contingent
turned slowly in the direction of their home
street.   They began to give, each to each,

distorted versions of the fight.   Causes of re-treat in particular cases were magnified. Blows dealt in the fight were enlarged to catapultian power, and stones thrown were alleged to have hurtled with infinite accuracy. Valor grew strong again, and the little boys began to swear with great spirit.

"Ah, we blokies kin lick deh hull damn Row," said a child, swaggering.

Little Jimmie was striving to stanch the flow of blood from his cut lips.   Scowling, he turned upon the speaker.

"Ah, where deh hell was yeh when I was doin' all deh fightin'?" he demanded.   "Youse kids makes me tired."

"Ah, go ahn," replied the other argumenta-tively.

Jimmie replied with heavy contempt.   "Ah, youse can't fight, Blue Billie !   I kin lick yeh wid one han'."

"Ah, go ahn," replied Billie again.

"Ah," said Jimmie threateningly.

"Ah," said the other in the same tone.

They struck at each other, clinched, and rolled over on the cobble stones.

"Smash 'im, Jimmie, kick deh damn guts out of 'im," yelled Pete, the lad with the chronic sneer, in tones of delight.

The small combatants pounded and kicked, scratched and tore. They began to weep and their curses struggled in their throats with sobs. The other little boys clasped their hands and wriggled their legs in excitement. They formed a bobbing circle about the pair.

A tiny spectator was suddenly agitated.

"Cheese it, Jimmy, cheese it! Here comes yer fader," he yelled.

The circle of little boys instantly parted. They drew away and waited in ecstatic awe for that which was about to happen. The two little boys fighting in the modes of four thousand years ago, did not hear the warning.

Up the avenue there plodded slowly a man

with sullen eyes. He was carrying a dinner pail and smoking an apple-wood pipe.

As he neared the spot where the little boys strove, he regarded them listlessly. But suddenly he roared an oath and advanced upon the rolling fighters.

"Here, you Jim, git up, now, while I belt yer life out, you damned disorderly brat."

He began to kick into the chaotic mass on the ground. The boy Billie felt a heavy boot strike his head. He made a furious effort and disentangled himself from Jimmie. He tottered away, damning.

Jimmie arose painfully from the ground and confronting his father, began to curse him. His parent kicked him. "Come home, now," he cried, "an' stop yer jawin', er I'll lam the everlasting head off yehs."

They departed. The man paced placidly along with the apple-wood emblem of serenity between his teeth. The boy followed a dozen feet in the rear. He swore luridly, for he felt that it was degradation for one who aimed to be some vague soldier, or a man of blood with a sort of sublime license, to be taken home by a father.

CHAPTER II.

Eventually they entered into a dark region where, from a careening building, a dozen gruesome doorways gave up loads of babies to the street and the gutter. A wind of early autumn raised yellow dust from cobbles and swirled it against an hundred windows. Long streamers of garments fluttered from fire-escapes. In all unhandy places there were buckets, brooms, rags and bottles. In the street infants played or fought with other infants or sat stupidly in the way of vehicles. Formidable women, with uncombed hair and disordered dress, gossiped while leaning on railings, or screamed in frantic quarrels. Withered persons, in curious postures of submission to something, sat smoking pipes in obscure corners. A thousand odors of cooking food came forth to the street. The building quivered and creaked from the weight of humanity stamping about in its bowels.

A small ragged girl dragged a red, bawling infant along the crowded ways. He was hanging back, baby-like, bracing his wrinkled, bare legs.

The little girl cried out: "Ah, Tommie, come ahn. Dere's Jimmie and fader. Don't be a-pullin' me back."

She jerked the baby's arm impatiently. He fell on his face, roaring. With a second jerk she pulled him to his feet, and they went on. With the obstinacy of his order, he protested against being dragged in a chosen direction. He made heroic endeavors to keep on his legs, denounce his sister and consume a bit of orange peeling which he chewed between the times of his infantile orations.

As the sullen-eyed man, followed by the blood-covered boy, drew near, the little girl burst into reproachful cries. "Ah, Jimmie, youse bin fightin' agin."

The urchin swelled distainfully.

"Ah, what deh hell, Mag.   See?"

The little girl upbraided him,   "Youse allus fightin', Jimmie, an' yeh knows it puts mudder out when yehs come home half dead, an' it's like we'll all get a poundin'."

She began to weep.   The babe threw back his head and roared at his prospects.

"Ah, what deh hell!" cried Jimmie.   "Shut up er I'll smack yer mout'.   See?"

As his sister continued her lamentations, he suddenly swore and struck her.   The little girl reeled and, recovering herself, burst into tears and quaveringly cursed him.   As she slowly retreated her brother advanced dealing her cuffs.   The father heard and turned about.

"Stop that, Jim, d'yeh hear?   Leave yer sister alone on the street.   It's like I can never beat any sense into yer damned wooden head."

The urchin raised his voice in defiance to

his parent and continued his attacks. The babe bawled tremendously, protesting with great violence. During his sister's hasty manœuvres, he was dragged by the arm.

Finally the procession plunged into one of the gruesome doorways. They crawled up dark stairways and along cold, gloomy halls. At last the father pushed open a door and they entered a lighted room in which a large woman was rampant.

She stopped in a career from a seething stove to a pan-covered table. As the father and children filed in she peered at them.

"Eh, what? Been fightin' agin, by Gawd!" She threw herself upon Jimmie. The urchin tried to dart behind the others and in the scuffle the babe, Tommie, was knocked down. He protested with his usual vehemence, because they had bruised his tender shins against a table leg.

The mother's massive shoulders heaved with anger. Grasping the urchin by the neck and shoulder she shook him until he rattled. She dragged him to an unholy sink, and, soaking a rag in water, began to scrub his lacerated face with it. Jimmie screamed in pain and tried to twist his shoulders out of the clasp of the huge arms.

The babe sat on the floor watching the scene, his face in contortions like that of a woman at a tragedy. The father, with a newly-ladened pipe in his mouth, crouched on a backless chair near the stove. Jimmie's cries annoyed him. He turned about and bellowed at his wife :

" Let the damned kid alone for a minute, will yeh, Mary? Yer allus poundin' 'im. When I come nights I can't git no rest 'cause yer allus poundin' a kid. Let up, d'yeh hear? Don't be allus poundin' a kid."

The woman's operations on the urchin instantly increased in violence. At last she tossed him to a corner where he limply lay cursing and weeping.

The wife put her immense hands on her hips and with a chieftain-like stride approached her husband.

" Ho," she said, with a great grunt of contempt. " An' what in the devil are you stickin' your nose for ?"

The babe crawled under the table and, turning, peered out cautiously. The ragged girl retreated and the urchin in the corner drew his legs carefully beneath him.

The man puffed his pipe calmly and put his great mudded boots on the back part of the stove.

" Go teh hell," he murmured, tranquilly.

The woman screamed and shook her fists before her husband's eyes. The rough yellow of her face and neck flared suddenly crimson. She began to howl.

He puffed imperturbably at his pipe for a time, but finally arose and began to look out at the window into the darkening chaos of back yards.

"You've been drinkin', Mary," he said. "You'd better let up on the bot', ol' woman, or you'll git done."

"You're a liar.   I ain't had a drop," she roared in reply.

They had a lurid altercation, in which they damned each other's souls with frequence.

The babe was staring out from under the table, his small face working in his excitement.

The ragged girl went stealthily over to the corner where the urchin lay.

"Are yehs hurted much, Jimmie?" she whispered timidly.

"Not a damn bit! See?" growled the little boy.

"Will I wash deh blood?"

"Naw!"

"Will I"—

"When I catch dat Riley kid I'll break 'is face! Dat's right! See?"

He turned his face to the wall as if resolved to grimly bide his time.

In the quarrel between husband and wife, the woman was victor. The man grabbed his hat and rushed from the room, apparently determined upon a vengeful drunk. She followed to the door and thundered at him as he made his way down stairs.

She returned and stirred up the room until her children were bobbing about like bubbles.

"Git outa deh way," she persistently bawled, waving feet with their dishevelled shoes near the heads of her children. She shrouded herself, puffing and snorting, in a cloud of steam at the stove, and eventually extracted a frying-pan full of potatoes that hissed.

She flourished it. "Come teh yer suppers, now," she cried with sudden exasperation. "Hurry up, now, er I'll help yeh !"

The children scrambled hastily. With prodigious clatter they arranged themselves at table. The babe sat with his feet dangling high from a precarious infant chair and gorged his small stomach. Jimmie forced, with feverish rapidity, the grease-enveloped pieces between his wounded lips. Maggie, with side glances of fear of interruption, ate like a small pursued tigress.

The mother sat blinking at them. She delivered reproaches, swallowed potatoes and drank from a yellow-brown bottle. After a time her mood changed and she wept as she carried little Tommie into another room and laid him to sleep with his fists doubled in an old quilt of faded red and green grandeur. Then she came and moaned by the stove. She rocked to and fro upon a chair, shedding tears and crooning miserably to the two children about their " poor mother " and " yer fader, damn 'is soul."

The little girl plodded between the table and the chair with a dish-pan on it. She tottered on her small legs beneath burdens of dishes.

Jimmie sat nursing his various wounds. He cast furtive glances at his mother. His practised eye perceived her gradually emerge from a muddled mist of sentiment until her brain burned in drunken heat. He sat breathless.

Maggie broke a plate.

The mother started to her feet as if propelled.

"Good Gawd," she howled. Her eyes glittered on her child with sudden hatred. The fervent red of her face turned almost to purple. The little boy ran to the halls, shrieking like a monk in an earthquake.

He floundered about in darkness until he found the stairs. He stumbled, panic-stricken, to the next floor. An old woman opened a door. A light behind her threw a flare on the urchin's quivering face.

"Eh, Gawd, child, what is it dis time ? Is yer fader beatin' yer mudder, or yer mudder beatin' yer fader?"

CHAPTER III.

Jimmie and the old woman listened long in the hall. Above the muffled roar of conversation, the dismal wailings of babies at night, the thumping of feet in unseen corridors and rooms, mingled with the sound of varied hoarse shoutings in the street and the rattling of wheels over cobbles, they heard the screams of the child and the roars of the mother die away to a feeble moaning and a subdued bass muttering.

The old woman was a gnarled and leathery personage who could don, at will, an expression of great virtue. She possessed a small music-box capable of one tune, and a collection of "God bless yehs" pitched in assorted keys of fervency. Each day she took a position upon the stones of Fifth Avenue, where she crooked her legs under her and crouched immovable and hideous, like an idol. She received daily a small sum in pennies. It was contributed, for the most part, by persons who did not make their homes in that vicinity.

Once, when a lady had dropped her purse on the sidewalk, the gnarled woman had grabbed it and smuggled it with great dexterity beneath her cloak. When she was arrested she had cursed the lady into a partial swoon, and with her aged limbs, twisted from rheumatism, had almost kicked the stomach out of a huge policeman whose conduct upon that occasion she referred to when she said : "The police, damn 'em."

"Eh, Jimmie, it's cursed shame," she said. "Go, now, like a dear an' buy me a can, an' if yer mudder raises 'ell all night yehs can sleep here."

Jimmie took a tendered tin-pail and seven pennies and departed. He passed into the side door of a saloon and went to the bar. Straining up on his toes he raised the pail and pennies as high as his arms would let him. He saw two hands thrust down and take them. Directly the same hands let down the filled pail and he left.

In front of the gruesome doorway he met a lurching figure. It was his father, swaying about on uncertain legs.

"Give me deh can. See?" said the man, threateningly.

"Ah, come off! I got dis can fer dat ol' woman an' it 'ud be dirt teh swipe it. See?" cried Jimmie.

The father wrenched the pail from the urchin. He grasped it in both hands and lifted it to his mouth. He glued his lips to the under edge and tilted his head. His hairy throat swelled until it seemed to grow near his chin. There was a tremendous gulping movement and the beer was gone.

The man caught his breath and laughed. He hit his son on the head with the empty pail. As it rolled clanging into the street,

Jimmie began to scream and kicked repeatedly at his father's shins.

"Look at deh dirt what yeh done me," he yelled. "Deh ol' woman 'ill be raisin' hell."

He retreated to the middle of the street, but the man did not pursue. He staggered toward the door.

"I'll club hell outa yeh when I ketch yeh," he shouted, and disappeared.

During the evening he had been standing against a bar drinking whiskies and declaring to all comers, confidentially: "My home reg'lar livin' hell! Damndes' place! Reg'lar hell! Why do I come an' drin' whisk' here thish way? 'Cause home reg'lar livin' hell!"

Jimmie waited a long time in the street and then crept warily up through the building. He passed with great caution the door of the gnarled woman, and finally stopped outside his home and listened.

He could hear his mother moving heavily about among the furniture of the room. She was chanting in a mournful voice, occasionally interjecting bursts of volcanic wrath at the father, who, Jimmie judged, had sunk down on the floor or in a corner.

"Why deh blazes don' chere try teh keep Jim from fightin'? I'll break yer jaw," she suddenly bellowed.

The man mumbled with drunken indifference. "Ah, wha' deh hell. W'a's odds? Wha' makes kick?"

"Because he tears 'is clothes, yeh damn fool," cried the woman in supreme wrath.

The husband seemed to become aroused. "Go teh hell," he thundered fiercely in reply. There was a crash against the door and something broke into clattering fragments. Jimmie partially suppressed a howl and darted down the stairway. Below he paused and listened. He heard howls and curses, groans and shrieks, confusingly in chorus as if a battle were raging. With all was the crash of splintering furniture. The eyes of the urchin glared in fear that one of them would discover him.

Curious faces appeared in door-ways, and whispered comments passed to and fro. " Ol' Johnson's raisin' hell agin."

Jimmie stood until the noises ceased and the other inhabitants of the tenement had all yawned and shut their doors. Then he crawled upstairs with the caution of an invader of a panther den. Sounds of labored breathing came through the broken door-panels. He pushed the door open and entered, quaking.

A glow from the fire threw red hues over the bare floor, the cracked and soiled plastering, and the overturned and broken furniture.

In the middle of the floor lay his mother asleep. In one corner of the room his father's limp body hung across the seat of a chair.

The urchin stole forward. He began to shiver in dread of awakening his parents. His mother's great chest was heaving painfully. Jimmie paused and looked down at her. Her face was inflamed and swollen from drinking. Her yellow brows shaded eye-lids that had grown blue. Her tangled hair tossed in waves over her forehead. Her mouth was set in the same lines of vindictive hatred that it had, perhaps, borne during the fight. Her bare, red arms were thrown out above her head in positions of exhaustion, something, mayhap, like those of a sated villain.

The urchin bended over his mother. He was fearful lest she should open her eyes, and the dread within him was so strong, that he could not forbear to stare, but hung as if fascinated over the woman's grim face.

Suddenly her eyes opened. The urchin found himself looking straight into that expression, which, it would seem, had the power to change his blood to salt. He howled piercingly and fell backward.

The woman floundered for a moment, tossed her arms about her head as if in combat, and again began to snore.

Jimmie crawled back in the shadows and waited. A noise in the next room had followed his cry at the discovery that his mother was awake. He grovelled in the gloom, the eyes from out his drawn face riveted upon the intervening door.

He heard it creak, and then the sound of a small voice came to him. " Jimmie ! Jimmie ! Are yehs dere ?" it whispered. The urchin started. The thin, white face of his sister looked at him from the door-way of the other room. She crept to him across the floor.

The father had not moved, but lay in the same death-like sleep. The mother writhed in uneasy slumber, her chest wheezing as if she were in the agonies of strangulation. Out at the window a florid moon was peering over dark roofs, and in the distance the waters of a river glimmered pallidly.

The small frame of the ragged girl was quivering. Her features were haggard from weeping, and her eyes gleamed from fear. She grasped the urchin's arm in her little trembling hands and they huddled in a corner. The eyes of both were drawn, by some force, to stare at the woman's face, for they thought she need only to awake and all fiends would come from below.

They crouched until the ghost-mists of dawn appeared at the window, drawing close to the panes, and looking in at the prostrate, heaving body of the mother.

CHAPTER IV.

The babe, Tommie, died. He went away
in a white, insignificant coffin, his small waxen
hand clutching a flower that the girl, Maggie,
had stolen from an Italian.

She and Jimmie lived.

The inexperienced fibres of the boy's eyes
were hardened at an early age. He became a
young man of leather. He lived some red
years without laboring. During that time his
sneer became chronic. He studied human
nature in the gutter, and found it no worse
than he thought he had reason to believe it.
He never conceived a respect for the world,
because he had begun with no idols that it had
smashed.

He clad his soul in armor by means of hap-
pening hilariously in at a mission church where
a man composed his sermons of "yous."

While they got warm at the stove, he told his hearers just where he calculated they stood with the Lord. Many of the sinners were impatient over the pictured depths of their degradation. They were waiting for soup-tickets.

A reader of words of wind-demons might have been able to see the portions of a dialogue pass to and fro between the exhorter and his hearers.

"You are damned," said the preacher. And the reader of sounds might have seen the reply go forth from the ragged people : "Where's our soup ?"

Jimmie and a companion sat in a rear seat and commented upon the things that didn't concern them, with all the freedom of English gentlemen. When they grew thirsty and went out their minds confused the speaker with Christ.

Momentarily, Jimmie was sullen with thoughts of a hopeless altitude where grew fruit. His companion said that if he should ever meet God he would ask for a million dollars and a bottle of beer.

Jimmie's occupation for a long time was to stand on street-corners and watch the world go by, dreaming blood-red dreams at the passing of pretty women. He menaced mankind at the intersections of streets.

On the corners he was in life and of life. The world was going on and he was there to perceive it

He maintained a belligerent attitude toward all well-dressed men. To him fine raiment was allied to weakness, and all good coats covered faint hearts. He and his order were kings, to a certain extent, over the men of untarnished clothes, because these latter dreaded, perhaps, to be either killed or laughed at.

Above all things he despised obvious Christians and ciphers with the chrisanthemums of aristocracy in their button-holes. He considered himself above both of these classes.

He was afraid of neither the devil nor the leader of society.

When he had a dollar in his pocket his satisfaction with existence was the greatest thing in the world.   So, eventually, he felt obliged to work.   His father died and his mother's years were divided up into periods of thirty days.

He became a truck driver.   He was given the charge of a pains-taking pair of horses and a large rattling truck.   He invaded the turmoil and tumble of the down-town streets and learned to breath maledictory defiance at the police who occasionally used to climb up, drag him from his perch and beat him.

In the lower part of the city he daily involved himself in hideous tangles.   If he and his team chanced to be in the rear he preserved a demeanor of serenity, crossing his legs and bursting forth into yells when foot passengers took dangerous dives beneath the noses of his champing horses.   He smoked his pipe calmly for he knew that his pay was marching on.

If in the front and the key-truck of chaos, he entered terrifically into the quarrel that was raging to and fro among the drivers on their high seats, and sometimes roared oaths and violently got himself arrested.

After a time his sneer grew so that it turned its glare upon all things. He became so sharp that he believed in nothing. To him the police were always actuated by malignant impulses and the rest of the world was composed, for the most part, of despicable creatures who were all trying to take advantage of him and with whom, in defense, he was obliged to quarrel on all possible occasions. He himself occupied a down-trodden position that had a private but distinct element of grandeur in its isolation.

The most complete cases of aggravated idiocy were, to his mind, rampant upon the front platforms of all of the street cars. At first his tongue strove with these beings, but he eventually was superior. He became immured like an African cow. In him grew a majestic contempt for those strings of street cars that followed him like intent bugs.

He fell into the habit, when starting on a long journey, of fixing his eye on a high and distant object, commanding his horses to begin, and then going into a sort of a trance of observation. Multitudes of drivers might howl in his rear, and passengers might load him with opprobrium, he would not awaken until some blue policeman turned red and began to frenziedly tear bridles and beat the soft noses of the responsible horses.

When he paused to contemplate the attitude of the police toward himself and his fellows, he believed that they were the only men in the city who had no rights. When driving about, he felt that he was held liable by the police for anything that might occur in the streets, and was the common prey of all energetic officials. In revenge, he resolved never to move out of the way of anything, until formidable circumstances, or a much larger man than himself forced him to it.

Foot-passengers were mere pestering flies with an insane disregard for their legs and his convenience. He could not conceive their maniacal desires to cross the streets. Their madness smote him with eternal amazement. He was continually storming at them from his throne. He sat aloft and denounced their frantic leaps, plunges, dives and straddles.

When they would thrust at, or parry, the noses of his champing horses, making them swing their heads and move their feet, disturbing a solid dreamy repose, he swore at the men as fools, for he himself could perceive that Providence had caused it clearly to be written, that he and his team had the unalienable right to stand in the proper path of the sun chariot, and if they so minded, obstruct its mission or take a wheel off.

And, perhaps, if the god-driver had an ungovernable desire to step down, put up his flame colored fists and manfully dispute the right of way, he would have probably been immediately opposed by a scowling mortal with two sets of very hard knuckles.

It is possible, perhaps, that this young man would have derided, in an axle-wide alley, the approach of a flying ferry boat. Yet he achieved a respect for a fire engine. As one charged toward his truck, he would drive fearfully upon a side-walk, threatening untold people with annihilation. When an engine would strike a mass of blocked trucks, splitting it into fragments, as a blow annihilates a cake of ice, Jimmie's team could usually be observed high and safe, with whole wheels, on the side-walk. The fearful coming of the engine could break up the most intricate muddle of heavy vehicles at which the police had been swearing for the half of an hour.

A fire-engine was enshrined in his heart as

an appalling thing that he loved with a distant dog-like devotion. They had been known to overturn street-cars. Those leaping horses, striking sparks from the cobbles in their forward lunge, were creatures to be ineffably admired. The clang of the gong pierced his breast like a noise of remembered war.

When Jimmie was a little boy, he began to be arrested. Before he reached a great age, he had a fair record.

He developed too great a tendency to climb down from his truck and fight with other drivers. He had been in quite a number of miscellaneous fights, and in some general barroom rows that had become known to the police. Once he had been arrested for assaulting a Chinaman. Two women in different parts of the city, and entirely unknown to each other, caused him considerable annoyance by breaking forth, simultaneously, at fateful intervals, into wailings about marriage and support and infants.

Nevertheless, he had, on a certain star-lit evening, said wonderingly and quite reverently : " Deh moon looks like hell, don't it?"

CHAPTER V.

The girl, Maggie, blossomed in a mud puddle. She grew to be a most rare and wonderful production of a tenement district, a pretty girl.

None of the dirt of Rum Alley seemed to be in her veins. The philosophers up-stairs, down-stairs and on the same floor, puzzled over it.

When a child, playing and fighting with gamins in the street, dirt disguised her. Attired in tatters and grime, she went unseen.

There came a time, however, when the young men of the vicinity said : "Dat Johnson goil is a puty good looker." About this period her brother remarked to her : "Mag, I'll tell yeh dis ! See ? Yeh've edder got teh go teh hell or go teh work !" Whereupon she went to work, having the feminine aversion of going to hell.

By a chance, she got a position in an establishment where they made collars and cuffs. She received a stool and a machine in a room where sat twenty girls of various shades of yellow discontent. She perched on the stool and treadled at her machine all day, turning out collars, the name of whose brand could be noted for its irrelevancy to anything in connection with collars. At night she returned home to her mother.

Jimmie grew large enough to take the vague position of head of the family. As incumbent of that office, he stumbled up-stairs late at night, as his father had done before him. He reeled about .the room, swearing at his relations, or went to sleep on the floor.

The mother had gradually arisen to that degree of fame that she could bandy words with her acquaintances among the police-justices. Court-officials called her by her first name.

When she appeared they pursued a course which had been theirs for months. They invariably grinned and cried out : "Hello, Mary, you here again ?" Her grey head wagged in many a court. She always besieged the bench with voluble excuses, explanations, apologies and prayers. Her flaming face and rolling eyes were a sort of familiar sight on the island. She measured time by means of sprees, and was eternally swollen and dishevelled.

One day the young man, Pete, who as a lad had smitten the Devil's Row urchin in the back of the head and put to flight the antagonists of his friend, Jimmie, strutted upon the scene. He met Jimmie one day on the street, promised to take him to a boxing match in Williamsburg, and called for him in the evening.

Maggie observed Pete.

He sat on a table in the Johnson home and dangled his checked legs with an enticing nonchalance. His hair was curled down over his forehead in an oiled bang. His rather pugged nose seemed to revolt from contact with a bristling moustache of short, wire-like hairs. His blue double-breasted coat, edged with black braid, buttoned close to a red puff tie, and his patent-leather shoes, looked like murder-fitted weapons.

His mannerisms stamped him as a man who had a correct sense of his personal superiority. There was valor and contempt for circum-stances in the glance of his eye. He waved his hands like a man of the world, who dismisses religion and philosophy, and says "Fudge." He had certainly seen everything and with each curl of his lip, he declared that it amounted to nothing. Maggie thought he must be a very elegant and graceful bar-tender.

He was telling tales to Jimmie.

Maggie watched him furtively, with half-closed eyes, lit with a vague interest.

"Hully gee! Dey makes me tired," he

said. " Mos' e'ry day some farmer comes in an' tries teh run deh shop. See? But deh gits t'rowed right out! I jolt dem right out in deh street before dey knows where dey is! See?"

" Sure," said Jimmie.

" Dere was a mug come in deh place deh odder day wid an idear he wus goin' teh own deh place! Hully gee, he wus goin' teh own deh place! I see he had a still on an' I didn' wanna giv'im no stuff, so I says: 'Git deh hell outa here an' don' make no trouble,' I says like dat! See? ' Git deh hell outa here an' don' make no trouble;' like dat. 'Git deh hell outa here,' I says. See?"

Jimmie nodded understandingly. Over his features played an eager desire to state the amount of his valor in a similiar crisis, but the narrator proceeded.

" Well, deh blokie he says : 'T'hell wid it! I ain' lookin' for no scrap,' he says (See?) 'but' he says, 'I'm spectable cit'zen an' I

wanna drink an' purtydamnsoon, too.' See?
' Deh hell,' I says. Like dat! ' Deh hell,' l
says. See? ' Don' make no trouble,' I says.
Like dat. ' Don' make no trouble.' See?
Den deh mug he squared off an' said he was
fine as silk wid his dukes (See?) an' he wanned
a drink damnquick. Dat's what he said.
See?"

"Sure," repeated Jimmie.

Pete continued. " Say, I jes' jumped deh bar
an' deh way I plunked dat blokie was great.
See? Dat's right! In deh jaw! See? Hully
gee, he t'rowed a spittoon true deh front windee.
Say, I taut I'd drop dead. But deh boss, he
comes in after an' he says, ' Pete, yehs done
jes' right! Yeh've gota keep order an' it's all
right.' See? ' It's all right,' he says. Dat's
what he said."

The two held a technical discussion.

" Dat bloke was a dandy," said Pete, in conclusion, " but he had'n' oughta made no
trouble. Dat's what I says teh dem : ' Don'

come in here an' make no trouble,' I says, like dat. 'Don' make no trouble.' See."

As Jimmie and his friend exchanged tales descriptive of their prowess, Maggie leaned back in the shadow. Her eyes dwelt wonderingly and rather wistfully upon Pete's face. The broken furniture, grimey walls, and general disorder and dirt of her home of a sudden appeared before her and began to take a potential aspect. Pete's aristocratic person looked as if it might soil. She looked keenly at him, occasionally, wondering if he was feeling contempt. But Pete seemed to be enveloped in reminiscence.

"Hully gee," said he, "dose mugs can't phase me. Dey knows I kin wipe up deh street wid any tree of dem."

When he said, "Ah, what deh hell," his voice was burdened with disdain for the inevitable and contempt for anything that fate might compel him to endure.

Maggie perceived that here was the beau

ideal of a man. Her dim thoughts were often searching for far away lands where, as God says, the little hills sing together in the morn-ing. Under the trees of her dream-gardens there had always walked a lover.

CHAPTER VI.

Pete took note of Maggie.

"Say, Mag, I'm stuck on yer shape. It's outa sight,' he said, parenthetically, with an affable grin.

As he became aware that she was listening closely, he grew still more eloquent in his descriptions of various happenings in his career. It appeared that he was invincible in fights.

"Why," he said, referring to a man with whom he had had a misunderstanding, "dat mug scrapped like a damn dago. Dat's right. He was dead easy. See? He tau't he was a scrapper! But he foun' out diff'ent! Hully gee."

He walked to and fro in the small room, which seemed then to grow even smaller and unfit to hold his dignity, the attribute of a supreme warrior. That swing of the shoulders

that had frozen the timid when he was but a lad had increased with his growth and education at the ratio of ten to one. It, combined with the sneer upon his mouth, told mankind that there was nothing in space which could appall him. Maggie marvelled at him and surrounded him with greatness. She vaguely tried to calculate the altitude of the pinnacle from which he must have looked down upon her.

"I met a chump deh odder day way up in deh city," he said. "I was goin' teh see a frien' of mine. When I was a-crossin' deh street deh chump runned plump inteh me, an' den he turns aroun' an' says, 'Yer insolen' ruffin,' he says, like dat. 'Oh, gee,' I says, 'oh, gee, go teh hell and git off deh eart',' I says, like dat. See? 'Go teh hell an' git off deh eart',' like dat. Den deh blokie he got wild. He says I was a contempt'ble scoun'el, er someting like dat, an' he says I was doom' teh everlastin' pe'dition an' all like dat. 'Gee,'

I says, 'gee! Deh hell I am,' I says. 'Deh hell I am,' like dat. An' den I slugged 'im. See?"

With Jimmie in his company, Pete departed in a sort of a blaze of glory from the Johnson home. Maggie, leaning from the window, watched him as he walked down the street.

Here was a formidable man who disdained the strength of world full of fists. Here was one who had contempt for brass-clothed power; one whose knuckles could defiantly ring against the granite of law. He was a knight.

The two men went from under the glimmering street-lamp and passed into shadows.

Turning, Maggie contemplated the dark, dust-stained walls, and the scant and crude furniture of her home. A clock, in a splintered and battered oblong box of varnished wood, she suddenly regarded as an abomination. She noted that it ticked raspingly. The almost vanished flowers in the carpet-pattern, she conceived to be newly hideous. Some faint attempts she had made with blue ribbon, to freshen the appearance of a dingy curtain, she now saw to be piteous.

She wondered what Pete dined on.

She reflected upon the collar and cuff factory. It began to appear to her mind as a dreary place of endless grinding. Pete's elegant occupation brought him, no doubt, into contact with people who had money and manners. It was probable that he had a large acquaintance of pretty girls. He must have great sums of money to spend.

To her the earth was composed of hardships and insults. She felt instant admiration for a man who openly defied it. She thought that if the grim angel of death should clutch his heart, Pete would shrug his shoulders and say : " Oh, ev'ryt'ing goes."

She anticipated that he would come again shortly. She spent some of her week's pay in the purchase of flowered cretonne for a lambrequin. She made it with infinite care and hung it to the slightly-careening mantel, over the stove, in the kitchen. She studied it with painful anxiety from different points in the room. She wanted it to look well on Sunday night when, perhaps, Jimmie's friend would come. On Sunday night, however, Pete did not appear.

Afterward the girl looked at it with a sense of humiliation. She was now convinced that Pete was superior to admiration for lambrequins.

A few evenings later Pete entered with fascinating innovations in his apparel. As she had seen him twice and he had different suits on each time, Maggie had a dim impression that his wardrobe was prodigiously extensive.

"Say, Mag," he said, "put on yer bes' duds Friday night an' I'll take yehs teh deh show. See?"

He spent a few moments in flourishing his clothes and then vanished, without having glanced at the lambrequin.

Over the eternal collars and cuffs in the factory Maggie spent the most of three days in making imaginary sketches of Pete and his daily environment. She imagined some half dozen women in love with him and thought he must lean dangerously toward an indefinite one, whom she pictured with great charms of person, but with an altogether contemptible disposition.

She thought he must live in a blare of pleasure. He had friends, and people who were afraid of him.

She saw the golden glitter of the place where Pete was to take her. An entertainment of many hues and many melodies where she was afraid she might appear small and mouse-colored.

Her mother drank whiskey all Friday morning. With lurid face and tossing hair she cursed and destroyed furniture all Friday afternoon. When Maggie came home at half-past six her mother lay asleep amidst the wreck of chairs and a table. Fragments of various household utensils were scattered about the floor. She had vented some phase of drunken fury upon the lambrequin. It lay in a bedraggled heap in the corner.

"Hah," she snorted, sitting up suddenly, "where deh hell yeh been? Why deh hell don' yeh come home earlier? Been loafin' 'round deh streets. Yer gettin' teh be a reg'lar devil."

When Pete arrived Maggie, in a worn black dress, was waiting for him in the midst of a floor strewn with wreckage. The curtain at the window had been pulled by a heavy hand and hung by one tack, dangling to and fro in the draft through the cracks at the sash. The knots of blue ribbons appeared like violated flowers. The fire in the stove had gone out. The displaced lids and open doors showed heaps of sullen grey ashes. The remnants of a meal, ghastly, like dead flesh, lay in a corner. Maggie's red mother, stretched on the floor, blasphemed and gave her daughter a bad name.

CHAPTER VII.

An orchestra of yellow silk women and bald-headed men on an elevated stage near the centre of a great green-hued hall, played a popular waltz. The place was crowded with people grouped about little tables. A battalion of waiters slid among the throng, carrying trays of beer glasses and making change from the inexhaustible vaults of their trousers pockets. Little boys, in the costumes of French chefs, paraded up and down the irregular aisles vending fancy cakes. There was a low rumble of conversation and a subdued clinking of glasses. Clouds of tobacco smoke rolled and wavered high in air about the dull gilt of the chandeliers.

The vast crowd had an air throughout of having just quitted labor. Men with calloused hands and attired in garments that showed the wear of an endless trudge for a living, smoked their pipes contentedly and spent five, ten, or perhaps fifteen cents for beer. There was a mere sprinkling of kid-gloved men who smoked cigars purchased elsewhere. The great body of the crowd was composed of people who showed that all day they strove with their hands. Quiet Germans, with maybe their wives and two or three children, sat listening to the music, with the expressions of happy cows. An occasional party of sailors from a war-ship, their faces pictures of sturdy health, spent the earlier hours of the evening at the small round tables. Very infrequent tipsy men, swollen with the value of their opinions, engaged their companions in earnest and confidential conversation. In the balcony, and here and there below, shone the impassive faces of women. The nationalities of the Bowery beamed upon the stage from all directions.

Pete aggressively walked up a side aisle and

took seats with Maggie at a table beneath the balcony.

" Two beehs ! "

Leaning back he regarded with eyes of superiority the scene before them.   This attitude affected Maggie strongly.   A man who could regard such a sight with indifference must be accustomed to very great things.

It was obvious that Pete had been to this place many times before, and was very familiar with it.   A knowledge of this fact made Maggie feel little and new.

He was extremely gracious and attentive. He displayed the consideration of a cultured gentleman who knew what was due.

" Say, what deh hell ? Bring deh lady a big glass ! What deh hell use is dat pony ? "

" Don't be fresh, now," said the waiter, with some warmth, as he departed.

" Ah, git off deh eart'," said Pete, after the other's retreating form.

Maggie perceived that Pete brought forth

all his elegance and all his knowledge of high-class customs for her benefit Her heart warmed as she reflected upon his condescension.

The orchestra of yellow silk women and bald-headed men gave vent to a few bars of anticipatory music and a girl, in a pink dress with short skirts, galloped upon the stage. She smiled upon the throng as if in acknowledgment of a warm welcome, and began to walk to and fro, making profuse gesticulations and singing, in brazen soprano tones, a song, the words of which were inaudible. When she broke into the swift rattling measures of a chorus some half tipsy men near the stage joined in the rollicking refrain and glasses were pounded rhythmically upon the tables. People leaned forward to watch her and to try to catch the words of the song. When she vanished there were long rollings of applause.

Obedient to more anticipatory bars, she reappeared amidst the half-suppressed cheering of the tipsy men. The orchestra plunged into dance music and the laces of the dancer fluttered and flew in the glare of gas jets. She divulged the fact that she was attired in some half dozen skirts. It was patent that any one of them would have proved adequate for the purpose for which skirts are intended. An occasional man bent forward, intent upon the pink stockings. Maggie wondered at the splendor of the costume and lost herself in calculations of the cost of the silks and laces.

The dancer's smile of stereotyped enthusiasm was turned for ten minutes upon the faces of her audience. In the finale she fell into some of those grotesque attitudes which were at the time popular among the dancers in the theatres up-town, giving to the Bowery public the phantasies of the aristocratic theatre-going public, at reduced rates.

"Say, Pete," said Maggie, leaning forward, "dis it great."

"Sure," said Pete, with proper complacence.

A ventriloquist followed the dancer. He held two fantastic dolls on his knees. He made them sing mournful ditties and say funny things about geography and Ireland.

"Do dose little men talk?" asked Maggie.

"Naw," said Pete, "it's some damn fake. See?"

Two girls, on the bills as sisters, came forth and sang a duet that is heard occasionally at concerts given under church auspices. They supplemented it with a dance which of course can never be seen at concerts given under church auspices.

After the duettists had retired, a woman of debatable age sang a negro melody. The chorus necessitated some grotesque waddlings supposed to be an imitation of a plantation darkey, under the influence, probably, of music and the moon. The audience was just enthusiastic enough over it to have her return and sing a sorrowful lay, whose lines told of a mother's love and a sweetheart who waited

and a young man who was lost at sea under
the most harrowing circumstances.   From the
faces of a score or so in the crowd, the self-
contained look faded.   Many heads were bent
forward with eagerness and sympathy. As the
last distressing sentiment of the piece was
brought forth, it was greeted by that kind of
applause which rings as sincere.

As a final effort, the singer rendered some
verses which described a vision of Britain being
annihilated by America, and Ireland bursting
her bonds.   A carefully prepared crisis was
reached in the last line of the last verse,
where the singer threw out her arms and cried,
"The star-spangled banner." Instantly a
great cheer swelled from the throats of the
assemblage of the masses.   There was a heavy
rumble of booted feet thumping the floor.
Eyes gleamed with sudden fire, and calloused
hands waved frantically in the air.

After a few moments' rest, the orchestra
played crashingly, and a small fat man burst

out upon the stage. He began to roar a song and stamp back and forth before the foot-lights, wildly waving a glossy silk hat and throwing leers, or smiles, broadcast. He made his face into fantastic grimaces until he looked like a pictured devil on a Japanese kite. The crowd laughed gleefully. His short, fat legs were never still a moment. He shouted and roared and bobbed his shock of red wig until the audience broke out in excited applause.

Pete did not pay much attention to the progress of events upon the stage. He was drinking beer and watching Maggie.

Her cheeks were blushing with excitement and her eyes were glistening. She drew deep breaths of pleasure. No thoughts of the atmosphere of the collar and cuff factory came to her.

When the orchestra crashed finally, they jostled their way to the sidewalk with the crowd. Pete took Maggie's arm and pushed a way for her, offering to fight with a man or two.

They reached Maggie's home at a late hour and stood for a moment in front of the gruesome doorway.

" Say, Mag," said Pete, " give us a kiss for takin' yeh teh deh show, will yer ? "

Maggie laughed, as if startled, and drew away from him.

" Naw, Pete," she said, " dat wasn't in it."

" Ah, what deh hell ? " urged Pete.

The girl retreated nervously.

" Ah, what deh hell ? " repeated he.

Maggie darted into the hall, and up the stairs. She turned and smiled at him, then disappeared.

Pete walked slowly down the street. He had something of an astonished expression upon his features. He paused under a lamp-post and breathed a low breath of surprise.

" Gawd," he said, " I wonner if I've been played fer a duffer."

CHAPTER VIII.

As thoughts of Pete came to Maggie's mind, she began to have an intense dislike for all of her dresses.

"What deh hell ails yeh? What makes yeh be allus fixin' and fussin'? Good Gawd," her mother would frequently roar at her.

She began to note, with more interest, the well-dressed women she met on the avenues. She envied elegance and soft palms. She craved those adornments of person which she saw every day on the street, conceiving them to be allies of vast importance to women.

Studying faces, she thought many of the women and girls she chanced to meet, smiled with serenity as though forever cherished and watched over by those they loved.

The air in the collar and cuff establishment strangled her. She knew she was gradually and surely shrivelling in the hot, stuffy room. The begrimed windows rattled incessantly from the passing of elevated trains. The place was filled with a whirl of noises and odors.

She wondered as she regarded some of the grizzled women in the room, mere mechanical contrivances sewing seams and grinding out, with heads bended over their work, tales of imagined or real girl-hood happiness, past drunks, the baby at home, and unpaid wages. She speculated how long her youth would endure. She began to see the bloom upon her cheeks as valuable.

She imagined herself, in an exasperating future, as a scrawny woman with an eternal grievance. Too, she thought Pete to be a very fastidious person concerning the appear-ance of women.

She felt she would love to see somebody entangle their fingers in the oily beard of the fat foreigner who owned the establishment.

He was a detestable creature.   He wore white
socks with low shoes.

He sat all day delivering orations, in the
depths of a cushioned chair.   His pocket-
book deprived them of the power of retort.

" What een hell do you sink I pie fife dolla
a week for?   Play?   No, py damn ! "

Maggie was anxious for a friend to whom
she could talk about Pete.   She would have
liked to discuss his amirable mannerisms with
a reliable mutual friend.   At home, she found
her mother often drunk and always raving.

It seems that the world had treated this
woman very badly, and she took a deep revenge
upon such portions of it as came within her
reach.   She broke furniture as if she were at
last getting her rights.   She swelled with virtuous indignation as she carried the lighter
articles of household use, one by one under
the shadows of the three gilt balls, where He-
brews chained them with chains of interest.

Jimmie came when he was oblgied to by

circumstances over which he had no control. His well-trained legs brought him staggering home and put him to bed some nights when he would rather have gone elsewhere.

Swaggering Pete loomed like a golden sun to Maggie. He took her to a dime museum where rows of meek freaks astonished her. She contemplated their deformities with awe and thought them a sort of chosen tribe.

Pete, raking his brains for amusement, discovered the Central Park Menagerie and the Museum of Arts. Sunday afternoons would sometimes find them at these places. Pete did not appear to be particularly interested in what he saw. He stood around looking heavy, while Maggie giggled in glee.

Once at the Menagerie he went into a trance of admiration before the spectacle of a very small monkey threatening to trash a cageful because one of them had pulled his tail and he had not wheeled about quickly enough to discover who did it. Ever after Pete knew that monkey by sight and winked at him, trying to induce him to fight with other and larger monkeys

At the Museum, Maggie said, "Dis is outa sight."

"Oh hell," said Pete, "wait till next summer an' I'll take yehs to a picnic."

While the girl wandered in the vaulted rooms, Pete occupied himself in returning stony stare for stony stare, the appalling scrutiny of the watch-dogs of the treasures. Occasionally he would remark in loud tones: "Dat jay has got glass eyes," and sentences of the sort. When he tired of this amusement he would go to the mummies and moralize over them.

Usually he submitted with silent dignity to all which he had to go through, but, at times, he was goaded into comment.

"What deh hell," he demanded once. "Look at all dese little jugs! Hundred jugs in a row! Ten rows in a case an' 'bout a t'ousand cases! What deh blazes use is dem?"

Evenings during the week he took her to see plays in which the brain-clutching heroine was rescued from the palatial home of her guardian, who is cruelly after her bonds, by the hero with the beautiful sentiments. The latter spent most of his time out at soak in pale-green snow storms, busy with a nickel-plated revolver, rescuing aged strangers from villains.

Maggie lost herself in sympathy with the wanderers swooning in snow storms beneath happy-hued church windows. And a choir within singing "Joy to the World." To Maggie and the rest of the audience this was transcendental realism. Joy always within, and they, like the actor, inevitably without. Viewing it, they hugged themselves in ecstastic pity of their imagined or real condition.

The girl thought the arrogance and granite-heartedness of the magnate of the play was very accurately drawn. She echoed the maledictions that the occupants of the gallery showered on this individual when his lines compelled him to expose his extreme selfishness.

Shady persons in the audience revolted from the pictured villainy of the drama. With untiring zeal they hissed vice and applauded virtue. Unmistakably bad men evinced an apparently sincere admiration for virtue.

The loud gallery was overwhelmingly with the unfortunate and the oppressed. They encouraged the struggling hero with cries, and jeered the villain, hooting and calling attention to his whiskers. When anybody died in the pale-green snow storms, the gallery mourned. They sought out the painted misery and hugged it as akin.

In the hero's erratic march from poverty in the first act, to wealth and triumph in the final one, in which he forgives all the enemies that he has left, he was assisted by the gallery, which applauded his generous and noble sentiments and confounded the speeches of his opponents by making irrelevant but very sharp remarks. Those actors who were cursed with villainy parts were confronted at every turn by the gallery. If one of them rendered lines containing the most subtile distinctions between right and wrong, the gallery was immediately aware if the actor meant wickedness, and denounced him accordingly.

The last act was a triumph for the hero, poor and of the masses, the representative of the audience, over the villain and the rich man, his pockets stuffed with bonds, his heart packed with tyrannical purposes, imperturbable amid suffering.

Maggie always departed with raised spirits from the showing places of the melodrama. She rejoiced at the way in which the poor and virtuous eventually surmounted the wealthy and wicked. The theater made her think. She wondered if the culture and refinement she had seen imitated, perhaps grotesquely, by the heroine on the stage, could be acquired by a girl who lived in a tenement house and worked in a shirt factory.

→ The poor overcome the rich

CHAPTER IX.

A group of urchins were intent upon the side door of a saloon. Expectancy gleamed from their eyes. They were twisting their fingers in excitement.

"Here she comes," yelled one of them suddenly.

The group of urchins burst instantly asunder and its individual fragments were spread in a wide, respectable half circle about the point of interest. The saloon door opened with a crash, and the figure of a woman appeared upon the threshold. He gray hair fell in knotted masses about her shoulders. Her face was crimsoned and wet with perspiration. Her eyes had a rolling glare.

"Not a damn cent more of me money will yehs ever get, not a damn cent. I spent me money here fer t'ree years an' now yehs tells me yeh'll sell me no more stuff! T'hell wid yeh, Johnnie Murckre! 'Disturbance?' Disturbance be damned! T'hell wid yeh, Johnnie—"

The door received a kick of exasperation from within and the woman lurched heavily out on the sidewalk.

The gamins in the half-circle became violently agitated. They began to dance about and hoot and yell and jeer. Wide dirty grins spread over each face.

The woman made a furious dash at a particularly outrageous cluster of little boys. They laughed delightedly and scampered off a short distance, calling out over their shoulders to her. She stood tottering on the curbstone and thundered at them.

"Yeh devil's kids," she howled, shaking red fists. The little boys whooped in glee. As she started up the street they fell in behind and marched uproariously. Occasionally she wheeled about and made charges on them.

They ran nimbly out of reach and taunted her.

In the frame of a gruesome doorway she stood for a moment cursing them. Her hair straggled, giving her crimson features a look of insanity. Her great fists quivered as she shook them madly in the air.

The urchins made terrific noises until she turned and disappeared. Then they filed quietly in the way they had come.

The woman floundered about in the lower hall of the tenement house and finally stumbled up the stairs. On an upper hall a door was opened and a collection of heads peered curiously out, watching her. With a wrathful snort the woman confronted the door, but it was slammed hastily in her face and the key was turned.

She stood for a few minutes, delivering a frenzied challenge at the panels.

"Come out in deh hall, Mary Murphy, damn yeh, if yehs want a row. Come ahn, yeh overgrown terrier, come ahn."

She began to kick the door with her great feet. She shrilly defied the universe to appear and do battle. Her cursing trebles brought heads from all doors save the one she threatened. Her eyes glared in every direction. The air was full of her tossing fists.

"Come ahn, deh hull damn gang of yehs, come ahn," she roared at the spectators. An oath or two, cat-calls, jeers and bits of facetious advice were given in reply. Missles clattered about her feet.

"What deh hell's deh matter wid yeh?" said a voice in the gathered gloom, and Jimmie came forward. He carried tin a dinner-pail in his hand and under his arm a brown truckman's apron done in a bundle. "What deh hell's wrong?" he demanded.

"Come out, all of yehs, come out," his mother was howling. "Come ahn an' I'll stamp yer damn brains under me feet."

"Shet yer face, an' come home, yer damned old fool," roared Jimmie at her. She strided up to him and twirled her fingers in his face. Her eyes were darting flames of unreasoning rage and her framed trembled with eagerness for a fight.

" T'hell wid yehs! An' who deh hell are yehs? I ain't givin' a snap of me fingers fer yehs," she bawled at him. She turned her huge back in tremendous disdain and climbed the stairs to the next floor.

Jimmie followed, cursing blackly. At the top of the flight he seized his mother's arm and started to drag her toward the door of their room.

"Come home, damn yeh," he gritted between his teeth.

" Take yer hands off me! Take yer hands off me," shrieked his mother.

She raised her arm and whirled her great fist at her son's face. Jimmie dodged his head and the blow struck him in the back of the neck. " Damn yeh," gritted he again. He threw out his left hand and writhed his fingers about her middle arm. The mother and the son began to sway and struggle like gladiators.

"Whoop!" said the Rum Alley tenement house. The hall filled with interested spectators.

"Hi, ol' lady, dat was a dandy!"

"T'ree to one on deh red!"

"Ah, stop yer dam scrappin'!"

The door of the Johnson home opened and Maggie looked out. Jimmie made a supreme cursing effort and hurled his mother into the room. He quickly followed and closed the door. The Rum Alley tenement swore disappointedly and retired.

The mother slowly gathered herself up from the floor. Her eyes glittered menacingly upon her children.

"Here, now," said Jimmie, "we've had enough of dis. Sit down, an' don' make no trouble."

He grasped her arm, and twisting it, forced her into a creaking chair.

" Keep yer hands off me," roared his mother again.

" Damn yer ol' hide," yelled Jimmie, madly. Maggie shrieked and ran into the other room. To her there came the sound of a storm of crashes and curses. There was a great final thump and Jimmie's voice cried : " Dere damn yeh, stay still." Maggie opened the now, door and went warily out. " Oh, Jimmie."

He was leaning against the wall and swearing. Blood stood upon bruises on his knotty fore-arms where they had scraped against the floor or the walls in the scuffle. The mother lay screeching on the floor, the tears running down her furrowed face.

Maggie, standing in the middle of the room, gazed about her. The usual upheaval of the tables and chairs had taken place. Crockery was strewn broadcast in fragments. The stove had been disturbed on its legs, and now leaned idiotically to one side.

A pail had been upset and water spread in all directions.

The door opened and Pete appeared. He shrugged his shoulders. "Oh, Gawd," he observed.

He walked over to Maggie and whispered in her ear. "Ah, what deh hell, Mag? Come ahn and we'll have a hell of a time."

The mother in the corner upreared her head and shook her tangled locks.

"Teh hell wid him and you," she said, glowering at her daughter in the gloom. Her eyes seemed to burn balefully. "Yeh've gone teh deh devil, Mag Johnson, yehs knows yehs have gone teh deh devil. Yer a disgrace teh yer people, damn yeh. An' now, git out an' go ahn wid dat doe-faced jude of yours. Go teh hell wid him, damn yeh, an' a good riddance. Go teh hell an' see how yeh likes it."

Maggie gazed long at her mother.

"Go teh hell now, an' see how yeh likes it. Git out. I won't have sech as yehs in me

prophesy

Prostitution

house !   Get out, d'yeh hear !   Damn yeh, git out !"

The girl began to tremble.

At this instant Pete came forward.   " Oh, what deh hell, Mag, see," whispered he softly in her ear.   " Dis all blows over.   See ?   Deh ol' woman 'ill be all right in deh mornin'.   Come ahn out wid me !   We'll have a hell of a time."

The woman on the floor cursed.   Jimmie was intent upon his bruised fore-arms.   The girl cast a glance about the room filled with a chaotic mass of debris, and at the red, writhing body of her mother.

" Go teh hell an' good riddance.

She went.

Mother kicks Maggie out

CHAPTER X.

Jimmie had an idea it wasn't common courtesy for a friend to come to one's home and ruin one's sister. But he was not sure how much Pete knew about the rules of politeness.

The following night he returned home from work at rather a late hour in the evening. In passing through the halls he came upon the gnarled and leathery old woman who possessed the music box. She was grinning in the dim light that drifted through dust-stained panes. She beckoned to him with a smudged forefinger.

"Ah, Jimmie, what do yehs tink I got onto las' night. It was deh funnies' ting I ever saw," she cried, coming close to him and leering. She was trembling with eagerness to tell her tale. "I was by me door las' night when yer sister and her jude feller came in late, oh, very late. An' she, the dear, she was a-cryin' as if her heart would break, she was. It was deh funnies' ting I ever saw. An' right out here by me door she asked him did he love her, did he. An' she was a-cryin' as if her heart would break, poor t'ing. An' him, I could see be deh way what he said it dat she had been askin' orften, he says : " Oh, hell, yes," he says, says he, " Oh, hell, yes."

Storm-clouds swept over Jimmie's face, but he turned from the leathery old woman and plodded on up stairs.

" Oh, hell, yes," called she after him. She laughed a laugh that was like a prophetic croak. " ' Oh, hell, yes,' he says, says he, ' Oh, hell, yes.' "

There was no one in at home. The rooms showed that attempts had been made at tidying them. Parts of the wreckage of the day before had been repaired by an unskilful hand. A chair or two and the table, stood uncertainly upon legs. The floor had been newly swept.

Too, the blue ribbons had been restored to the curtains, and the lambrequin, with its immense sheaves of yellow wheat and red roses of equal size, had been returned, in a worn and sorry state, to its position at the mantel. Maggie's jacket and hat were gone from the nail behind the door.

Jimmie walked to the window and began to look through the blurred glass. It occurred to him to vaguely wonder, for an instant, if some of the women of his acquaintance had brothers.

Suddenly, however, he began to swear.

"But he was me frien'! I brought 'im here! Dat's deh hell of it!"

He fumed about the room, his anger gradually rising to the furious pitch.

"I'll kill deh jay! Dat's what I'll do! I'll kill deh jay!"

He clutched his hat and sprang toward the door. But it opened and his mother's great form blocked the passage.

"What deh hell's deh matter wid yeh?" exclaimed she, coming into the rooms.

Jimmie gave vent to a sardonic curse and then laughed heavily.

"Well, Maggie's gone teh deh devil! Dat's what! See?"

"Eh?" said his mother.

"Maggie's gone teh deh devil! Are yehs deaf?" roared Jimmie, impatiently.

"Deh hell she has," murmured the mother, astounded.

Jimmie grunted, and then began to stare out at the window. His mother sat down in a chair, but a moment later sprang erect and delivered a maddened whirl of oaths. Her son turned to look at her as she reeled and swayed in the middle of the room, her fierce face convulsed with passion, her blotched arms raised high in imprecation.

"May Gawd curse her forever," she shrieked. "May she eat nothin' but stones and deh dirt in deh street. May she sleep in deh gutter an' never see deh sun shine agin. Deh damn—"

"Here, now," said her son. "Take a drop on yourself."

The mother raised lamenting eyes to the ceiling.

"She's deh devil's own chil', Jimmie," she whispered. "Ah, who would tink such a bad girl could grow up in our fambly, Jimmie, me son. Many deh hour I've spent in talk wid dat girl an' tol' her if she ever went on deh streets I'd see her damned. An' after all her bringin' up an' what I tol' her and talked wid her, she goes teh deh bad, like a duck teh water."

The tears rolled down her furrowed face. Her hands trembled.

"An' den when dat Sadie MacMallister next door to us was sent teh deh devil by dat feller what worked in deh soap-factory, didn't I tell our Mag dat if she—"

"Ah, dat's anudder story," interrupted the

brother. "Of course, dat Sadie was nice an'
all dat—but—see—it ain't dessame as if—well,
Maggie was diff'ent—see—she was diff'ent."

He was trying to formulate a theory that
he had always unconsciously held, that all
sisters, excepting his own, could advisedly be
ruined.

He suddenly broke out again. "I'll go
t'ump hell outa deh mug what did her deh
harm. I'll kill 'im ! He tinks he kin scrap, but
when he gits me a-chasin' 'im he'll fin' out
where he's wrong, deh damned duffer. I'll
wipe up deh street wid 'im.

In a fury he plunged out of the doorway.
As he vanished the mother raised her head
and lifted both hands, entreating.

" May Gawd curse her forever," she cried.

In the darkness of the hallway Jimmie discerned a knot of women talking volubly.
When he strode by they paid no attention to
him.

" She allus was a bold thing," he heard one

of them cry in an eager voice. "Dere wasn't a feller come teh deh house but she'd try teh mash 'im. My Annie says deh shameless t'ing tried teh ketch her feller, her own feller, what we useter know his fader."

"I could a' tol' yehs dis two years ago," said a woman, in a key of triumph. "Yesir, it was over two years ago dat I says teh my ol' man, I says, 'Dat Johnson girl ain't straight,' I says. 'Oh, hell,' he says. 'Oh, hell.' 'Dat's all right,' I says, 'but I know what I knows,' I says, 'an' it'ill come out later. You wait an' see,' I says, 'you see.'"

"Anybody what had eyes could see dat dere was somethin' wrong wid dat girl. I didn't like her actions."

On the street Jimmie met a friend. "What deh hell?" asked the latter.

Jimmie explained. "An' I'll tump 'im till he can't stand."

"Oh, what deh hell," said the friend. "What's deh use!" Yeh'll git pulled in!

Everybody 'ill be onto it! An' ten plunks! Gee!"

Jimmie was determined. "He t'inks he kin scrap, but he'll fin' out diff'ent."

"Gee," remonstrated the friend, "What deh hell?"

CHAPTER XI.

On a corner a glass-fronted building shed a yellow glare upon the pavements. The open mouth of a saloon called seductively to passengers to enter and annihilate sorrow or create rage.

The interior of the place was papered in olive and bronze tints of imitation leather. A shining bar of counterfeit massiveness extended down the side of the room. Behind it a great mahogany-appearing sideboard reached the ceiling. Upon its shelves rested pyramids of shimmering glasses that were never disturbed. Mirrors set in the face of the sideboard multiplied them. Lemons, oranges and paper napkins, arranged with mathematical precision, sat among the glasses. Many-hued decanters of liquor perched at regular intervals on the lower shelves. A nickel-plated cash register occupied a position in the exact center of the general effect. The elementary senses of it all seemed to be opulence and geometrical accuracy.

Across from the bar a smaller counter held a collection of plates upon which swarmed frayed fragments of crackers, slices of boiled ham, dishevelled bits of cheese, and pickles swimming in vinegar. An odor of grasping, begrimmed hands and munching mouths pervaded.

Pete, in a white jacket, was behind the bar bending expectantly toward a quiet stranger. "A beeh," said the man. Pete drew a foam-topped glassful and set it dripping upon the bar.

At this moment the light bamboo doors at the entrance swung open and crashed against the siding. Jimmie and a companion entered. They swaggered unsteadily but belligerently toward the bar and looked at Pete with bleared and blinking eyes.

" Gin," said Jimmie.

"Gin," said the companion.

Pete slid a bottle and two glasses along the bar. He bended his head sideways as he assiduously polished away with a napkin at the gleaming wood. He had a look of watchfulness upon his features.

Jimmie and his companion kept their eyes upon the bartender and conversed loudly in tones of contempt.

" He's a dindy masher, ain't he, by Gawd ? " laughed Jimmie.

"Oh, hell, yes," said the companion, sneering widely. " He's great, he is. Git onto deh mug on deh blokie. Dat's enough to make a feller turn hand-springs in 'is sleep."

The quiet stranger moved himself and his glass a trifle further away and maintained an attitude of oblivion.

" Gee ! ain't he hot stuff ! "

"Git onto his shape ! Great Gawd ! "

" Hey," cried Jimmie, in tones of command.

Pete came along slowly, with a sullen dropping of the under lip.

"Well," he growled, "what's eatin' yehs?"

"Gin," said Jimmie.

"Gin," said the companion.

As Pete confronted them with the bottle and the glasses, they laughed in his face. Jimmie's companion, evidently overcome with merriment, pointed a grimy forefinger in Pete's direction.

"Say, Jimmie," demanded he, "what deh hell is dat behind deh bar?"

"Damned if I knows," replied Jimmie. They laughed loudly. Pete put down a bottle with a bang and turned a formidable face toward them. He disclosed his teeth and his shoulders heaved restlessly.

"You fellers can't guy me," he said. "Drink yer stuff an' git out an' don' make no trouble."

Instantly the laughter faded from the faces of the two men and expressions of offended dignity immediately came.

" Who deh hell has said anyt'ing teh you,"
cried they in the same breath.

The quiet stranger looked at the door cal-
culatingly.

"Ah, come off," said Pete to the two men.
" Don't pick me up for no jay. Drink yer rum
an' git out an' don' make no trouble."

"Oh, deh hell," airily cried Jimmie.

"Oh, deh hell," airily repeated his companion.

"We goes when we git ready! See!" continued Jimmie.

"Well," said Pete in a threatening voice,
"don' make no trouble."

Jimmie suddenly leaned forward with his
head on one side. He snarled like a wild
animal.

"Well, what if we does? See?" said he.

Dark blood flushed into Pete's face, and he
shot a lurid glance at Jimmie.

"Well, den we'll see whose deh bes' man,
you or me," he said.

The quiet stranger moved modestly toward the door.

Jimmie began to swell with valor.

"Don' pick me up fer no tenderfoot. When yeh tackles me yeh tackles one of deh bes' men in deh city. See? I'm a scrapper, I am. Ain't dat right, Billie?

"Sure, Mike," responded his companion in tones of conviction.

"Oh, hell," said Pete, easily. "Go fall on yerself."

The two men again began to laugh.

"What deh hell is dat talkin?" cried the companion.

"Damned if I knows," replied Jimmie with exaggerated contempt.

Pete made a furious gesture. "Git outa here now, an' don' make no trouble. See? Youse fellers er lookin' fer a scrap an' it's damn likely yeh'll fin' one if yeh keeps on shootin' off yer mout's. I know yehs! See? I kin lick better men dan yehs ever saw in yer lifes. Dat's right ! See? Don' pick me up fer no stuff er yeh might be jolted out in deh street before yeh knows where yeh is. When I comes from behind dis bar, I t'rows yehs boat inteh deh street. See ?"

" Oh, hell," cried the two men in chorus.

The glare of a panther came into Pete's eyes " Dat's what I said ! Unnerstan' ? "

He came through a passage at the end of the bar and swelled down upon the two men. They stepped promptly forward and crowded close to him.

They bristled like three roosters. They moved their heads pugnaciously and kept their shoulders braced. The nervous muscles about each mouth twitched with a forced smile of mockery.

" Well, what deh hell yer goin' teh do ? " gritted Jimmie.

Pete stepped warily back, waving his hand before him to keep the men from coming too near.

"Well, what deh hell yer goin' teh do?" re-peated Jimmie's ally. They kept close to him, taunting and leering. They strove to make him attempt the initial blow.

"Keep back, now! Don' crowd me," omin-ously said Pete.

Again they chorused in contempt. "Oh, hell!"

In a small, tossing group, the three men edged for positions like frigates contem-plating battle.

"Well, why deh hell don' yeh try teh t'row us out?" cried Jimmie and his ally with copi-ous sneers.

The bravery of bull-dogs sat upon the faces of the men. Their clenched fists moved like eager weapons.

The allied two jostled the bartender's elbows, glaring at him with feverish eyes and forcing him toward the wall.

Suddenly Pete swore redly. The flash of action gleamed from his eyes. He threw back his arm and aimed a tremendous, lightning-like blow at Jimmie's face. His foot swung a step forward and the weight of his body was behind his fist. Jimmie ducked his head, Bowery-like, with the quickness of a cat. The fierce, answering blows of him and his ally crushed on Pete's bowed head.

The quiet stranger vanished.

The arms of the combatants whirled in the air like flails. The faces of the men, at first flushed to flame-colored anger, now began to fade to the pallor of warriors in the blood and heat of a battle. Their lips curled back and stretched tightly over the gums in ghoul-like grins. Through their white, gripped teeth struggled hoarse whisperings of oaths. Their eyes glittered with murderous fire.

Each head was huddled between its owner's shoulders, and arms were swinging with marvelous rapidity. Feet scraped to and fro with a loud scratching sound upon the sanded floor. Blows left crimson blotches upon pale skin.

The curses of the first quarter minute of the fight died away. The breaths of the fighters came wheezingly from their lips and the three chests were straining and heaving. Pete at intervals gave vent to low, labored hisses, that sounded like a desire to kill. Jimmie's ally gibbered at times like a wounded maniac. Jimmie was silent, fighting with the face of a sacrificial priest. The rage of fear shone in all their eyes and their blood-colored fists swirled.

At a tottering moment a blow from Pete's hand struck the ally and he crashed to the floor. He wriggled instantly to his feet and grasping the quiet stranger's beer glass from the bar, hurled it at Pete's head.

High on the wall it burst like a bomb, shivering fragments flying in all directions. Then missles came to every man's hand. The place had heretofore appeared free of things to throw, but suddenly glass and bottles went singing through the air. They were thrown point blank at bobbing heads. The pyramid of shimmering glasses, that had never been disturbed, changed to cascades as heavy bottles were flung into them. Mirrors splintered to nothing.

The three frothing creatures on the floor buried themseives in a frenzy for blood. There followed in the wake of missles and fists some unknown prayers, perhaps for death.

The quiet stranger had sprawled very pyrotechnically out on the sidewalk. A laugh ran up and down the avenue for the half of a block.

"Dey've trowed a bloke inteh deh street."

People heard the sound of breaking glass and shuffling feet within the saloon and came running. A small group, bending down to look under the bamboo doors, watching the fall of glass, and three pairs of violent legs, changed in a moment to a crowd.

A policeman came charging down the side-walk and bounced through the doors into the saloon. The crowd bended and surged in absorbing anxiety to see.

Jimmie caught first sight of the on-coming interruption. On his feet he had the same regard for a policeman that, when on his truck, he had for a fire engine. He howled and ran for the side door.

The officer made a terrific advance, club in hand. One comprehensive sweep of the long night stick threw the ally to the floor and forced Pete to a corner. With his disengaged hand he made a furious effort at Jimmie's coat-tails. Then he regained his balance and paused.

"Well, well, you are a pair of pictures. What in hell yeh been up to?"

Jimmie, with his face drenched in blood, escaped up a side street, pursued a short distance by some of the more law-loving, or excited individuals of the crowd.

Later, from a corner safely dark, he saw the policeman, the ally and the bartender emerge from the saloon. Pete locked the doors and then followed up the avenue in the rear of the crowd-encompassed policeman and his charge.

On first thoughts Jimmie, with his heart throbbing at battle heat, started to go des· perately to the rescue of his friend, but he halted.

"Ah, what deh hell?" he demanded of himself.

CHAPTER XII.

In a hall of irregular shape sat Pete and Maggie drinking beer. A submissive orchestra dictated to by a spectacled man with frowsy hair and a dress suit, industriously followed the bobs of his head and the waves of his baton. A ballad singer, in a dress of flaming scarlet, sang in the inevitable voice of brass. When she vanished, men seated at the tables near the front applauded loudly, pounding the polished wood with their beer glasses. She returned attired in less gown, and sang again. She received another enthusiastic encore. She reappeared in still less gown and danced. The deafening rumble of glasses and clapping of hands that followed her exit indicated an overwhelming desire to have her come on for the fourth time, but the curiosity of the audience was not gratified.

Maggie was pale. From her eyes had been plucked all look of self-reliance. She leaned with a dependent air toward her companion. She was timid, as if fearing his anger or displeasure. She seemed to beseech tenderness of him.

[handwritten margin note: Maggie becomes dependent]

Pete's air of distinguished valor had grown upon him until it threatened stupendous dimensions. He was infinitely gracious to the girl. It was apparent to her that his condescension was a marvel.

He could appear to strut even while sitting still and he showed that he was a lion of lordly characteristics by the air with which he spat.

With Maggie gazing at him wonderingly, he took pride in commanding the waiters who were, however, indifferent or deaf.

" Hi, you, git a russle on yehs ! What deh hell yeh's lookin' at ? Two more beehs, d'yeh hear ?"

He leaned back and critically regarded the person of a girl with a straw-colored wig who upon the stage was flinging her heels in somewhat awkward imitation of a well-known danseuse.

At times Maggie told Pete long confidential tales of her former home life, dwelling upon the escapades of the other members of the family and the difficulties she had to combat in order to obtain a degree of comfort. He responded in tones of philanthropy. He pressed her arm with an air of reassuring proprietorship.

" Dey was damn jays," he said, denouncing the mother and brother.

The sound of the music which, by the efforts of the frowsy-headed leader, drifted to her ears through the smoked-filled atmosphere, made the girl dream. She thought of her former Rum Alley environment and turned to regard Pete's strong protecting fists. She thought of the collar and cuff manufactory and the eternal moan of the proprietor : " What een hell do you sink I pie fife dolla a week for? Play? No, py damn." She contemplated Pete's man-subduing eyes and noted that wealth and prosperity was indicated by his clothes. She imagined a future, rose-tinted, because of its distance from all that she previously had experienced.

As to the present she perceived only vague reasons to be miserable. Her life was Pete's and she considered him worthy of the charge. She would be disturbed by no particular apprehensions, so long as Pete adored her as he now said he did. She did not feel like a bad woman. To her knowledge she had never seen any better.

At times men at other tables regarded the girl furtively. Pete, aware of it, nodded at her and grinned. He felt proud.

"Mag, yer a bloomin' good-looker," he remarked, studying her face through the haze. The men made Maggie fear, but she blushed at Pete's words as it became apparent to her that she was the apple of his eye.

Grey-headed men, wonderfully pathetic in their dissipation, stared at her through clouds. Smooth cheeked boys, some of them with faces of stone and mouths of sin, not nearly so pathetic as the grey heads, tried to find the girl's eyes in the smoke wreaths. Maggie considered she was not what they thought her. She confined her glances to Pete and the stage.

The orchestra played negro melodies and a versatile drummer pounded, whacked, clattered and scratched on a dozen machines to make noise.

Those glances of the men, shot at Maggie from under half-closed lids, made her tremble. She thought them all to be worse men than Pete.

"Come, let's go," she said.

As they went out Maggie perceived two women seated at a table with some men. They were painted and their cheeks had lost their roundness. As she passed them the girl, with a shrinking movement, drew back her skirts.

CHAPTER XIII.

Jimmie did not return home for a number of days after the fight with Pete in the saloon. When he did, he approached with extreme caution.

He found his mother raving. Maggie had not returned home The parent continually wondered how her daughter could come to such a pass. She had never considered Maggie as a pearl dropped unstained into Rum Alley from Heaven, but she could not conceive how it was possible for her daughter to fall so low as to bring disgrace upon her family. She was terrific in denunciation of the girl's wickedness.

The fact that the neighbors talked of it, maddened her. When women came in, and in the course of their conversation casually asked, "Where's Maggie dese days?" the mother shook her fuzzy head at them and appalled them with curses. Cunning hints inviting confidence she rebuffed with violence.

"An' wid all deh bringin' up she had, how could she?" moaningly she asked of her son. "Wid all deh talkin' wid her I did an' deh t'ings I tol' her to remember? When a girl is bringed up deh way I bringed up Maggie, how kin she go teh deh devil?"

Jimmie was transfixed by these questions. He could not conceive how under the circumstances his mother's daughter and his sister could have been so wicked.

His mother took a drink from a squdgy bottle that sat on the table. She continued her lament.

"She had a bad heart, dat girl did, Jimmie. She was wicked teh deh heart an' we never knowed it."

Jimmie nodded, admitting the fact.

"We lived in deh same house wid her an' I

brought her up an' we never knowed how bad she was."

Jimmie nodded again.

" Wid a home like dis an' a mudder like me, she went teh deh bad," cried the mother, raising her eyes.

One day, Jimmie came home, sat down in a chair and began to wriggle about with a new and strange nervousness. At last he spoke shamefacedly.

" Well, look-a-here, dis t'ing queers us ! See ? We're queered ! An' maybe it 'ud be better if I—well, I t'ink I kin look 'er up an'— maybe it 'ud be better if I fetched her home an—"

The mother started from her chair and broke forth into a storm of passionate anger.

" What !   Let 'er come an' sleep under deh same roof wid her mudder agin ! Oh, yes, I will, won't I ? Sure ? Shame on yehs, Jimmie Johnson, fer sayin' such a t'ing teh yer own mudder—teh yer own mudder ! Little

did I tink when yehs was a babby playin' about
me feet dat ye'd grow up teh say sech a t'ing
teh yer mudder—yer own mudder. I never
taut—"

Sobs choked her and interrupted her reproaches.

" Dere ain't nottin teh raise sech hell about,"
said Jimmie. " I on'y says it 'ud be better if
we keep dis t'ing dark, see? It queers us!
See?"

His mother laughed a laugh that seemed to
ring through the city and be echoed and re-
echoed by countless other laughs. "Oh, yes,
I will, wont I! Sure!"

" Well, yeh must take me fer a damn fool,"
said Jimmie, indignant at his mother for mocking him. " I didn't say we'd make 'er inteh a
little tin angel, ner nottin, but deh way
it is now she can queer us! Don' che
see?"

" Aye, she'll git tired of deh life atter a
while an' den she'll wanna be a-comin' home,

won' she, deh beast! I'll let 'er in den, won' I ?"

"Well, I didn' mean none of dis prod'gal bus'ness anyway, explained Jimmie.

"It wasn't no prod'gal dauter, yeh damn fool," said the mother. "It was prod'gal son, anyhow."

"I know dat," said Jimmie.

For a time they sat in silence. The mother's eyes gloated on a scene her imagination could call before her. Her lips were set in a vindictive smile.

"Aye, she'll cry, won' she, an' carry on, an' tell how Pete, or some odder feller, beats 'er an' she'll say she's sorry an' all dat an' she ain't happy, she ain't, an' she wants to come home agin, she does."

With grim humor, the mother imitated the possible wailing notes of the daughter's voice.

"Den I'll take 'er in, won't I, deh beast. She kin cry 'er two eyes out on deh stones of deh street before I'll dirty deh place wid her. She abused an' ill-treated her own mudder—her own mudder what loved her an' she'll never git anodder chance dis side of hell."

Jimmie thought he had a great idea of women's frailty, but he could not understand why any of his kin should be victims.

"Damn her," he fervidly said.

Again he wondered vaguely if some of the women of his acquaintance had brothers. Nevertheless, his mind did not for an instant confuse himself with those brothers nor his sister with theirs. After the mother had, with great difficulty, suppressed the neighbors, she went among them and proclaimed her grief. "May Gawd forgive dat girl," was her continual cry. To attentive ears she recited the whole length and breadth of her woes.

"I bringed 'er up deh way a dauter oughta be bringed up an' dis is how she served me! She went teh deh devil deh first chance she got! May Gawd forgive her."

When arrested for drunkenness she used

the story of her daughter's downfall with telling effect upon the police justices. Finally one of them said to her, peering down over his spectacles : " Mary, the records of this and other courts show that you are the mother of forty-two daughters who have been ruined. The case is unparalleled in the annals of this court, and this court thinks—"

The mother went through life shedding large tears of sorrow. Her red face was a picture of agony.

Of course Jimmie publicly damned his sister that he might appear on a higher social plane. But, arguing with himself, stumbling about in ways that he knew not, he, once, almost came to a conclusion that his sister would have been more firmly good had she better known why. However, he felt that he could not hold such a view. He threw it hastily aside.

CHAPTER XIV.

In a hilarious hall there were twenty-eight tables and twenty-eight women and a crowd of smoking men. Valiant noise was made on a stage at the end of the hall by an orchestra composed of men who looked as if they had just happened in. Soiled waiters ran to and fro, swooping down like hawks on the unwary in the throng; clattering along the aisles with trays covered with glasses; stumbling over women's skirts and charging two prices for everything but beer, all with a swiftness that blurred the view of the cocoanut palms and dusty monstrosities painted upon the walls of the room. A bouncer, with a immense load of business upon his hands, plunged about in the crowd, dragging bashful strangers to prominent chairs, ordering waiters here and there and quarreling furiously with men who wanted to sing with the orchestra.

The usual smoke cloud was present, but so dense that heads and arms seemed entangled in it. The rumble of conversation was replaced by a roar. Plenteous oaths heaved through the air. The room rang with the shrill voices of women bubbling o'er with drink-laughter. The chief element in the music of the orchestra was speed. The musicians played in intent fury. A woman was singing and smiling upon the stage, but no one took notice of her. The rate at which the piano, cornet and violins were going, seemed to impart wildness to the half-drunken crowd. Beer glasses were emptied at a gulp and conversation became a rapid chatter. The smoke eddied and swirled like a shadowy river hurrying toward some unseen falls. Pete and Maggie entered the hall and took chairs at a table near the door. The woman who was seated there made an attempt to occupy Pete's attention and, failing, went away.

Three weeks had passed since the girl had

now they're enveloped in smoke

left home.   The air of spaniel-like dependence had been magnified and showed its direct effect in the peculiar off-handedness and ease of Pete's ways toward her.

She followed Pete's eyes with hers, anticipating with smiles gracious looks from him.

A woman of brilliance and audacity, accompanied by a mere boy, came into the place and took seats near them.

At once Pete sprang to his feet, his face beaming with glad surprise.

" By Gawd, there's Nellie," he cried.

He went over to the table and held out an eager hand to the woman.

" Why, hello, Pete, me boy, how are you," said she, giving him her fingers.

Maggie took instant note of the woman. She perceived that her black dress fitted her to perfection.   Her linen collar and cuffs were spotless.   Tan gloves were stretched over her well-shaped hands.   A hat of a prevailing fashion perched jauntily upon her dark hair.   She wore no jewelry and was painted with no apparent paint.   She looked clear-eyed through the stares of the men.

"Sit down, and call your lady-friend over," she said cordially to Pete.   At his beckoning Maggie came and sat between Pete and the mere boy.

"I thought yeh were gone away fer good," began Pete, at once.   "When did yeh git back?   How did dat Buff'lo bus'ness turn out?"

The woman shrugged her shoulders.   "Well, he didn't have as many stamps as he tried to make out, so I shook him, that's all."

"Well, I'm glad teh see yehs back in deh city," said Pete, with awkward gallantry.

He and the woman entered into a long conversation, exchanging reminiscences of days together.   Maggie sat still, unable to formulate an intelligent sentence upon the conversation and painfully aware of it.

She saw Pete's eyes sparkle as he gazed

upon the handsome stranger. He listened smilingly to all she said. The woman was familiar with all his affairs, asked him about mutual friends, and knew the amount of his salary.

She paid no attention to Maggie, looking toward her once or twice and apparently seeing the wall beyond.

The mere boy was sulky. In the beginning he had welcomed with acclamations the additions.

" Let's all have a drink ! What'll you take, Nell ? And you, Miss what's-your-name. Have a drink, Mr. ——, you, I mean."

He had shown a sprightly desire to do the talking for the company and tell all about his family. In a loud voice he declaimed on various topics. He assumed a patronizing air toward Pete. As Maggie was silent, he paid no attention to her. He made a great show of lavishing wealth upon the woman of brilliance and audacity.

" Do keep still, Freddie ! You gibber like an ape, dear," said the woman to him. She turned away and devoted her attention to Pete.

" We'll have many a good time together again, eh ?"

" Sure, Mike," said Pete, enthusiastic at once.

"Say," whispered she, leaning forward, "let's go over to Billie's and have a heluva time."

" Well, it's dis way! See ?" said Pete. " I got dis lady frien' here."

" Oh, t'hell with her," argued the woman.

Pete appeared disturbed.

" All right," said she, nodding her head at him. " All right for you ! We'll see the next time you ask me to go anywheres with you."

Pete squirmed.

" Say," he said, beseechingly, " come wid me a minit an' I'll tell yer why."

The woman waved her hand.

"Oh, that's all right, you needn't explain, you know. You wouldn't come merely because you wouldn't come, that's all there is of it."

To Pete's visible distress she turned to the mere boy, bringing him speedily from a terrific rage. He had been debating whether it would be the part of a man to pick a quarrel with Pete, or would he be justified in striking him savagely with his beer glass without warning. But he recovered himself when the woman turned to renew her smilings. He beamed upon her with an expression that was somewhat tipsy and inexpressibly tender.

"Say, shake that Bowery jay," requested he, in a loud whisper.

"Freddie, you are so droll," she replied.

Pete reached foward and touched the woman on the arm.

"Come out a minit while I tells yeh why I can't go wid yer. Yer doin' me dirt, Nell! I never taut ye'd do me dirt, Nell. Come on, will yer?" He spoke in tones of injury.

"Why, I don't see why I should be interested in your explanations," said the woman, with a coldness that seemed to reduce Pete to a pulp.

His eyes pleaded with her. "Come out a minit while I tells yeh."

The woman nodded slightly at Maggie and the mere boy, "Scuse me."

The mere boy interrupted his loving smile and turned a shriveling glare upon Pete. His boyish countenance flushed and he spoke, in a whine, to the woman:

"Oh, I say, Nellie, this ain't a square deal, you know. You aren't goin' to leave me and go off with that dufter, are you? I should think—"

"Why, you dear boy, of course I'm not," cried the woman, affectionately. She bended over and whispered in his ear. He smiled again and settled in his chair as if resolved to wait patiently.

As the woman walked down between the rows of tables, Pete was at her shoulder talking earnestly, apparently in explanation. The woman waved her hands with studied airs of indifference. The doors swung behind them, leaving Maggie and the mere boy seated at the table.

Maggie was dazed. She could dimly perceive that something stupendous had happened. She wondered why Pete saw fit to remonstrate with the woman, pleading for forgiveness with his eyes. She thought she noted an air of submission about her leonine Pete. She was astounded.

The mere boy occupied himself with cocktails and a cigar. He was tranquilly silent for half an hour. Then he bestirred himself and spoke.

"Well," he said, sighing, "I knew this was the way it would be." There was another stillness. The mere boy seemed to be musing.

"She was pulling m'leg. That's the whole

amount of it," he said, suddenly. "It's a bloomin' shame the way that girl does. Why, I've spent over two dollars in drinks to-night. And she goes off with that plug-ugly who looks as if he had been hit in the face with a coin-dye. I call it rocky treatment for a fellah like me. Here, waiter, bring me a cock-tail and make it damned strong."

Maggie made no reply. She was watching the doors. "It's a mean piece of business," complained the mere boy. He explained to her how amazing it was that anybody should treat him in such a manner. "But I'll get square with her, you bet. She won't get far ahead of yours truly, you know," he added, winking. "I'll tell her plainly that it was bloomin' mean business. And she won't come it over me with any of her 'now-Freddie-dears.' She thinks my name is Freddie, you know, but of course it ain't. I always tell these people some name like that, because if they got onto your right name they might use it sometime.   Understand? Oh, they don't fool me much."

Maggie was paying no attention, being intent upon the doors.   The mere boy relapsed into a period of gloom, during which he exterminated a number of cock-tails with a determined air, as if replying defiantly to fate.   He occasionally broke forth into sentences composed of invectives joined together in a long string.

The girl was still staring at the doors. After a time the mere boy began to see cobwebs just in front of his nose.   He spurred himself into being agreeable and insisted upon her having a charlotte-russe and a glass of beer.

"They's gone," he remarked, "they's gone." He looked at her through the smoke wreaths. "Shay, lil' girl, we mightish well make bes' of it.   You ain't such bad lookin' girl, y'know. Not half bad.   Can't come up to Nell, though. No, can't do it!   Well, I should shay not! Nell fine-lookin' girl!   F—i—n—ine.   You look damn bad longsider her, but by y'self ain't so bad. Have to do anyhow. Nell gone O'ny you left. Not half bad, though."

Maggie stood up.

"I'm going home," she said.

The mere boy started.

"Eh? What? Home," he cried, struck with amazement. "I beg pardon, did hear say home?"

"I'm going home," she repeated.

"Great Gawd, what hava struck," demanded the mere boy of himself, stupefied.

In a semi-comatose state he conducted her on board an up-town car, ostentatiously paid her fare, leered kindly at her through the rear window and fell off the steps.

CHAPTER XV.

A forlorn woman went along a lighted avenue. The street was filled with people desperately bound on missions. An endless crowd darted at the elevated station stairs and the horse cars were thronged with owners of bundles.

The pace of the forlorn woman was slow. She was apparently searching for some one. She loitered near the doors of saloons and watched men emerge from them. She scanned furtively the faces in the rushing stream of pedestrians. Hurrying men, bent on catching some boat or train, jostled her elbows, failing to notice her, their thoughts fixed on distant dinners.

The forlorn woman had a peculiar face. Her smile was no smile. But when in repose her features had a shadowy look that was like a sardonic grin, as if some one had sketched with cruel forefinger indelible lines about her mouth.

Jimmie came strolling up the avenue. The woman encountered him with an aggrieved air.

"Oh, Jimmie, I've been lookin' all over fer yehs—," she began.

Jimmie made an impatient gesture and quickened his pace.

"Ah, don't bodder me! Good Gawd!" he said, with the savageness of a man whose life is pestered.

The woman followed him along the sidewalk in somewhat the manner of a suppliant.

"But, Jimmie," she said, "yehs told me ye'd—"

Jimmie turned upon her fiercely as if resolved to make a last stand for comfort and peace.

"Say, fer Gawd's sake, Hattie, don' foller me from one end of deh city teh deh odder. Let up, will yehs! Give me a minute's res',

can't yehs?   Yehs makes me tired, allus tag-
gin' me.   See?   Ain' yehs got no sense?   Do
yehs want people teh get onto me?   Go chase
yerself, fer Gawd's sake."

The woman stepped closer and laid her
fingers on his arm.   "But, look-a here—"

Jimmie snarled.   "Oh, go teh hell."

He darted into the front door of a con-
venient saloon and a moment later came out
into the shadows that surrounded the side
door.   On the brilliantly lighted avenue he
perceived the forlorn woman dodging about
like a scout.   Jimmie laughed with an air of
relief and went away.

When he arrived home he found his mother
clamoring.   Maggie had returned.   She stood
shivering beneath the torrent of her mother's
wrath.

"Well, I'm damned," said Jimmie in greet-
ing.

His mother, tottering about the room,
pointed a quivering fore-finger.

"Lookut her, Jimmie, lookut her. Dere's yer sister, boy. Dere's yer sister. Lookut her! Lookut her!"

She screamed in scoffing laughter.

The girl stood in the middle of the room. She edged about as if unable to find a place on the floor to put her feet.

"Ha, ha, ha," bellowed the mother. "Dere she stands! Ain' she purty? Lookut her! Ain' she sweet, deh beast? Lookut her! Ha, ha, lookut her!"

She lurched forward and put her red and seamed hands upon her daughter's face. She bent down and peered keenly up into the eyes of the girl.

"Oh, she's jes' dessame as she ever was, ain' she? She's her mudder's purty darlin' yit, ain' she? Lookut her, Jimmie! Come here, fer Gawd's sake, and lookut her."

The loud, tremendous sneering of the mother brought the denizens of the Rum Alley tenement to their doors. Women came in the hall-ways. Children scurried to and fro.

"What's up? Dat Johnson party on anud-der tear?"

"Naw! Young Mag's come home!"

"Deh hell yeh say?"

Through the open doors curious eyes stared in at Maggie. Children ventured into the room and ogled her, as if they formed. the front row at a theatre. Women, without, bended toward each other and whispered, nod-ding their heads with airs of profound philoso-phy. A baby, overcome with curiosity con-cerning this object at which all were looking, sidled forward and touched her dress, cautious-ly, as if investigating a red-hot stove. Its mother's voice rang out like a warning trumpet. She rushed forward and grabbed her child, casting a terrible look of indignation at the girl.

Maggie's mother paced to and fro, address-ing the doorful of eyes, expounding like a glib

showman at a museum. Her voice rang
through the building.

"Dere she stands," she cried, wheeling suddenly and pointing with dramatic finger.
"Dere she stands!   Lookut her!   Ain' she a
dindy? An' she was so good as to come home
teh her mudder, she was!   Ain' she a beaut'?
Ain' she a dindy?   Fer Gawd's sake!"

The jeering cries ended in another burst of
shrill laughter.

The girl seemed to awaken.   "Jimmie—"

He drew hastily back from her

"Well, now, yer a hell of a t'ing, ain' yeh?"
he said, his lips curling in scorn.   Radiant
virtue sat upon his brow and his repelling
hands expressed horror of contamination.

Maggie turned and went.

The crowd at the door fell back precipitately.
A baby falling down in front of the door,
wrenched a scream like a wounded animal
from its mother.   Another woman sprang forward and picked it up, with a chivalrous air, as

if rescuing a human being from an oncoming express train.

As the girl passed down through the hall, she went before open doors framing more eyes strangely microscopic, and sending broad beams of inquisitive light into the darkness of her path. On the second floor she met the gnarled old woman who possessed the music box.

"So," she cried, "'ere yehs are back again, are yehs? An' dey've kicked yehs out? Well, come in an' stay wid me teh-night. I ain' got no moral standin'."

From above came an unceasing babble of tongues, over all of which rang the mother's derisive laughter.

CHAPTER XVI.

Pete did not consider that he had ruined Maggie. If he had thought that her soul could never smile again, he would have believed the mother and brother, who were pyrotechnic over the affair, to be responsible for it.

Besides, in his world, souls did not insist upon being able to smile. "What deh hell?"

He felt a trifle entangled. It distressed him. Revelations and scenes might bring upon him the wrath of the owner of the saloon, who insisted upon respectability of an advanced type.

"What deh hell do dey wanna' raise such a smoke about it fer? demanded he of himself, disgusted with the attitude of the family. He saw no necessity for anyone's losing their equilibrium merely because their sister or their daughter had stayed away from home.

Searching about in his mind for possible reasons for their conduct, he came upon the conclusion that Maggie's motives were correct, but that the two others wished to snare him. He felt pursued.

The woman of brilliance and audacity whom he had met in the hilarious hall showed a disposition to ridicule him.

"A little pale thing with no spirit," she said. "Did you note the expression of her eyes? There was something in them about pumpkin pie and virtue. That is a peculiar way the left corner of her mouth has of twitching, isn't it? Dear, dear, my cloud-compelling Pete, what are you coming to?"

Pete asserted at once that he never was very much interested in the girl. The woman interrupted him, laughing.

"Oh, it's not of the slightest consequence to me, my dear young man. You needn't draw maps for my benefit. Why should I be concerned about it?"

But Pete continued with his explanations. If he was laughed at for his tastes in women, he felt obliged to say that they were only temporary or indifferent ones.

The morning after Maggie had departed from home, Pete stood behind the bar. He was immaculate in white jacket and apron and his hair was plastered over his brow with infinite correctness. No customers were in the place. Pete was twisting his napkined fist slowly in a beer glass, softly whistling to himself and occasionally holding the object of his attention between his eyes and a few weak beams of sunlight that had found their way over the thick screens and into the shaded room.

With lingering thoughts of the woman of brilliance and audacity, the bartender raised his head and stared through the varying cracks between the swaying bamboo doors. Suddenly the whistling pucker faded from his lips. He saw Maggie walking slowly past.

He gave a great start, fearing for the pre-viously-mentioned eminent respectability of the place.

He threw a swift, nervous glance about him, all at once feeling guilty.   No one was in the room.

He went hastily over to the side door. Opening it and looking out, he perceived Maggie standing, as if undecided, on the cor-ner.   She was searching the place with her eyes.

As she turned her face toward him Pete beckoned to her hurriedly, intent upon return-ing with speed to a position behind the bar and to the atmosphere of respectability upon which the proprietor insisted.

Maggie came to him, the anxious look dis-appearing from her face and a smile wreathing her lips.

" Oh, Pete—," she began brightly.

The bartender made a violent gesture of impatience.

"Oh, my Gawd," cried he, vehemently. "What deh hell do yeh wanna hang aroun' here fer? Do yeh wanna git me inteh trouble?" he demanded with an air of injury.

Astonishment swept over the girl's features. "Why, Pete! yehs tol' me—"

Pete glanced profound irritation. His countenance reddened with the anger of a man whose respectability is being threatened.

"Say, yehs makes me tired. See? What deh hell deh yeh wanna tag aroun' atter me fer? Yeh'll git me inteh trouble wid deh ol' man an' dey'll be hell teh pay! If he sees a woman roun' here he'll go crazy an' I'll lose me job! See? Ain' yehs got no sense? Don' be allus bodderin' me. See? Yer brudder come in here an' raised hell an' deh ol' man hada put up fer it! An' now I'm done! See? I'm done."

The girl's eyes stared into his face. "Pete, don' yeh remem—"

"Oh, hell," interrupted Pete, anticipating.

The girl seemed to have a struggle with herself. She was apparently bewildered and could not find speech. Finally she asked in a low voice: "But where kin I go?"

The question exasperated Pete beyond the powers of endurance. It was a direct attempt to give him some responsibility in a matter that did not concern him. In his indignation he volunteered information.

"Oh, go teh hell," cried he. He slammed the door furiously and returned, with an air of relief, to his respectability.

Maggie went away.

She wandered aimlessly for several blocks. She stopped once and asked aloud a question of herself: "Who?"

A man who was passing near her shoulder, humorously took the questioning word as intended for him.

"Eh? What? Who? Nobody! I did'nt say anything," he laughingly said, and continued his way.

Soon the girl discovered that if she walked with such apparent aimlessness, some men looked at her with calculating eyes. She quickened her step, frightened. As a protection, she adopted a demeanor of intentness as if going somewhere.

After a time she left rattling avenues and passed between rows of houses with sterness and stolidity stamped upon their features. She hung her head for she felt their eyes grimly upon her.

Suddenly she came upon a stout gentleman in a silk hat and a chaste black coat, whose decorous row of buttons reached from his chin to his knees. The girl had heard of the Grace of God and she decided to approach this man.

His beaming, chubby face was a picture of benevolence and kind-heartedness. His eyes shone good-will.

But as the girl timidly accosted him, he gave a convulsive movement and saved his respectability by a vigorous side-step. He did not risk it to save a soul. For how was he to know that there was a soul before him that needed saving?

CHAPTER XVII.

Upon a wet evening, several months after the last chapter two interminable rows of cars, pulled by slipping horses, jangled along a prominent side-street. A dozen cabs, with coat-enshrouded drivers, clattered to and fro. Electric lights, whirring softly, shed a blurred radiance. A flower dealer, his feet tapping impatiently, his nose and his wares glistening with rain-drops, stood behind an array of roses and chrysanthemums. Two or three theatres emptied a crowd upon the storm-swept pavements. Men pulled their hats over their eyebrows and raised their collars to their ears. Women shrugged impatient shoulders in their warm cloaks and stopped to arrange their skirts for a walk through the storm. People having been comparatively silent for two hours burst into a roar of conversation, their hearts still kindling from the glowings of the stage.

The pavements became tossing seas of umbrellas. Men stepped forth to hail cabs or cars, raising their fingers in varied forms of polite request or imperative demand. An endless procession wended toward elevated stations. An atmosphere of pleasure and prosperity seemed to hang over the throng, born, perhaps, of good clothes and of having just emerged from a place of forgetfulness.

In the mingled light and gloom of an adjacent park, a handful of wet wanderers, in attitudes of chronic dejection, was scattered among the benches.

A girl of the painted cohorts of the city went along the street. She threw changing glances at men who passed her, giving smiling invitations to men of rural or untaught pattern and usually seeming sedately unconscious of the men with a metropolitan seal upon their faces.

Crossing glittering avenues, she went into the throng emerging from the places of forgetness. She hurried forward through the crowd as if intent upon reaching a distant home, bending forward in her handsome cloak, daintily lifting her skirts and picking for her well-shod feet the dryer spots upon the pavements.

The restless doors of saloons, clashing to and fro, disclosed animated rows of men before bars and hurrying barkeepers.

A concert hall gave to the street faint sounds of swift, machine-like music, as if a group of phantom musicians were hastening.

A tall young man, smoking a cigarette with a sublime air, strolled near the girl. He had on evening dress, a moustache, a chrysanthemum, and a look of ennui, all of which he kept carefully under his eye. Seeing the girl walk on as if such a young man as he was not in existence, he looked back transfixed with interest. He stared glassily for a moment, but gave a slight convulsive start when he discerned that she was neither new, Parisian, nor theatrical. He wheeled about hastily and turned his stare into the air, like a sailor with a search-light.

A stout gentleman, with pompous and philanthropic whiskers, went stolidly by, the broad of his back sneering at the girl.

A belated man in business clothes, and in haste to catch a car, bounced against her shoulder. " Hi, there, Mary, I beg your pardon ! Brace up, old girl." He grasped her arm to steady her, and then was away running down the middle of the street.

The girl walked on out of the realm of restaurants and saloons. She passed more glittering avenues and went into darker blocks than those where the crowd travelled.

A young man in light overcoat and derby hat received a glance shot keenly from the eyes of the girl. He stopped and looked at her, thrusting his hands in his pockets and making a mocking smile curl his lips. "Come, now, old lady," he said, "you don't mean to tell me that you sized me up for a farmer?"

A laboring man marched along with bundles under his arms. To her remarks, he replied: "It's a fine evenin', ain't it?"

She smiled squarely into the face of a boy who was hurrying by with his hand buried in his overcoat, his blonde locks bobbing on his youthful temples, and a cheery smile of unconcern upon his lips. He turned his head and smiled back at her, waving his hands.

"Not this eve—some other eve!"

A drunken man, reeling in her pathway, began to roar at her. "I ain' ga no money, dammit," he shouted, in a dismal voice. He lurched on up the street, wailing to himself, "Dammit, I ain' ga no money. Damn ba' luck. Ain' ga no more money."

The girl went into gloomy districts near the river, where the tall black factories shut in the street and only occasional broad beams of light fell across the pavements from saloons. In front of one of these places, from whence came the sound of a violin vigorously scraped, the patter of feet on boards and the ring of loud laughter, there stood a man with blotched features.

"Ah, there," said the girl.

"I've got a date," said the man.

Further on in the darkness she met a ragged being with shifting, blood-shot eyes and grimey hands. "Ah, what deh hell? Tink I'm a millionaire?"

She went into the blackness of the final block. The shutters of the tall buildings were closed like grim lips. The structures seemed to have eyet that looked over her, beyond her, at other things. Afar off the lights of the avenues glittered as if from an impossible distance. Street car bells jingled with a sound of merriment.

When almost to the river the girl saw a great figure. On going forward she perceived it to be a huge fat man in torn and greasy garments. His grey hair straggled down over his forehead. His small, bleared eyes, sparkling from amidst great rolls of red fat, swept eagerly over the girl's upturned face. He laughed, his brown, disordered teeth gleaming under a grey, grizzled moustache from which beer-drops dripped. His whole body gently quivered and shook like that of a dead jelly fish. Chuckling and leering, he followed the girl of the crimson legions.

At their feet the river appeared a deathly black hue. Some hidden factory sent up a yellow glare, that lit for a moment the waters lapping oilily against timbers. The varied sounds of life, made joyous by distance and seeming unapproachableness, came faintly and died away to a silence.

She heard no more

CHAPTER XVIII.

In a partitioned-off section of a saloon sat a man with a half dozen women, gleefully laughing, hovering about him. The man had arrived at that stage of drunkenness where affection is felt for the universe.

" I'm good f'ler, girls," he said, convincingly. " I'm damn good f'ler. An'body treats me right, I allus trea's zem right! See?"

The women nodded their heads approvingly. "To be sure," they cried in hearty chorus. "You're the kind of a man we like, Pete. You're outa sight! What yeh goin' to buy this time, dear?"

"An'thin' yehs wants, damn it," said the man in an abandonment of good will. His countenance shone with the true spirit of benevolence. He was in the proper mode of missionaries. He would have fraternized with obscure Hottentots. And above all, he was overwhelmed in tenderness for his friends, who were all illustrious.

"An'thing yehs wants, damn it," repeated he, waving his hands with beneficent recklessness. "I'm good f'ler, girls, an' if an'body treats me right I—here," called he through an open door to a waiter, "bring girls drinks, damn it. What 'ill yehs have, girls? An'thing yehs want, damn it!"

The waiter glanced in with the disgusted look of the man who serves intoxicants for the man who takes too much of them. He nodded his head shortly at the order from each indi-vidual, and went.

"Damn it," said the man, "we're havin' heluva time. I like you girls! Damn'd if I don't! Yer right sort! See?"

He spoke at length and with feeling, con-cerning the excellencies of his assembled friends.

"Don' try pull man's leg, but have a heluva

time ! Das right ! Das way teh do ! Now, if
I sawght yehs tryin' work me fer drinks,
wouldn' buy damn t'ing ! But yer right sort,
damn it ! Yehs know how ter treata a f'ler,
an' I stays by yehs 'til spen' las' cent ! Das
right ! I'm good f'ler an' I knows when
an'body treats me right !"

Between the times of the arrival and depar-
ture of the waiter, the man discoursed to the
women on the tender regard he felt for all
living things. He laid stress upon the purity
of his motives in all dealings with men in the
world and spoke of the fervor of his friendship
for those who were amiable. Tears welled
slowly from his eyes. His voice quavered
when he spoke to them.

Once when the waiter was about to depart
with an empty tray, the man drew a coin from
his pocket and held it forth.

"Here," said he, quite magnificently "here's
quar'."

The waiter kept his hands on his tray.

"I don' want yer money," he said.

The other put forth the coin with tearful insistence.

"Here, damn it," cried he, "tak't! Yer damn goo' f'ler an' I wan' yehs tak't!"

"Come, come, now," said the waiter, with the sullen air of a man who is forced into giving advice. "Put yer mon in yer pocket! Yer loaded an' yehs on'y makes a damn fool of yerself."

As the latter passed out of the door the man turned pathetically to the women.

"He don' know I'm damn goo' f'ler," cried he, dismally.

"Never you mind, Pete, dear," said a woman of brilliance and audacity, laying her hand with great affection upon his arm. "Never you mind, old boy! We'll stay by you, dear!"

"Das ri'," cried the man, his face lighting up at the soothing tones of the woman's voice. "Das ri', I'm damn goo' f'ler an' w'en anyone trea's me' ri', I treats zem ri'! Shee!"

" Sure !" cried the women.   " And we're not goin' back on you, old man."

The man turned appealing eyes to the woman of brilliance and audacity.   He felt that if he could be convicted of a contemptible action he would die.

" Shay, Nell, damn it, I allus trea's yehs shquare, didn' I ?   I allus been goo' f'ler wi' yehs, ain't I, Nell ? "

" Sure you have, Pete," assented the woman. She delivered an oration to her companions. " Yessir, that's a fact.   Pete's a square fellah, he is.   He never goes back on a friend.   He's the right kind an' we stay by him, don't we, girls ? "

" Sure," they exclaimed.   Looking lovingly at him they raised their glasses and drank his health.

" Girlsh," said the man, beseechingly, " I allus trea's yehs ri', didn' I ?   I'm goo' f'ler, ain' I, girlsh ? "

" Sure." again they chorused.

"Well," said he finally, "le's have nozzer drink, zen."

"That's right," hailed a woman, "that's right.   Yer no bloomin' jay!   Yer spends yer money like a man.   Dat's right."

The man pounded the table with his quiver-ering fists.

"Yessir," he cried, with deep earnestness, as if someone disputed him.   "I'm damn goo' f'ler, an' w'en anyone trea's me ri', I allus trea's —le's have nozzer drink."

He began to beat the wood with his glass.

"Shay," howled he, growing suddenly im-patient.   As the waiter did not then come, the man swelled with wrath.

"Shay," howled he again.

The waiter appeared at the door.

"Bringsh drinksh," said the man.

The waiter disappeared with the orders.

"Zat f'ler dam fool," cried the man.   "He insul' me!   I'm ge'man!   Can' stan' be insul'! I'm goin' lickim when comes!"

"No, no," cried the women, crowding about and trying to subdue him. "He's all right! He didn't mean anything! Let it go! He's a good fellah!"

"Din' he insul' me?" asked the man earnestly.

"No," said they. "Of course he didn't? He's all right!"

"Sure he didn' insul' me," demanded the man, with deep anxiety in his voice.

"No, no! We know him! He's a good fellah. He didn't mean anything."

"Well, zen," said the man, resolutely, "I'm go' 'pol'gize!"

When the waiter came, the man struggled to the middle of the floor.

"Girlsh shed you insul' me! I shay damn lie! I 'pol'gize!"

"All right," said the waiter.

The man sat down. He felt a sleepy but strong desire to straighten things out and have a perfect understanding with everybody.

"Nell, I allus trea's yeh shquare, din I? Yeh likes me, don' yehs, Nell? I'm goo' f'ler?"

"Sure," said the woman of brilliance and audacity.

"Yeh knows I'm stuck on yehs, don' yehs, Nell?"

"Sure," she repeated, carelessly.

Overwhelmed by a spasm of drunken adoration, he drew two or three bills from his pocket, and, with the trembling fingers of an offering priest, laid them on the table before the woman.

"Yehs knows, damn it, yehs kin have all got, 'cause I'm stuck on yehs, Nell, damn't, I—I'm stuck on yehs, Nell—buy drinksh—damn't— we're havin' heleva time—w'en anyone trea's me ri'—I—damn't, Nell—we're havin' heluva— time."

Shortly he went to sleep with his swollen face fallen forward on his chest.

The women drank and laughed, not heeding

the slumbering man in the corner. Finally he lurched forward and fell groaning to the floor.

The women screamed in disgust and drew back their skirts.

" Come ahn," cried one, starting up angrily, " let's get out of here."

The woman of brilliance and audacity stayed behind, taking up the bills and stuffing them into a deep, irregularly-shaped pocket. A gut-tural snore from the recumbent màn caused her to turn and look down at him.

She laughed. " What a damn fool," she said, and went.

The smoke from the lamps settled heavily down in the little compartment, obscuring the way out. The smell of oil, stifling in its intensity, pervaded the air. The wine from an overturned glasss dripped softly down upon the blotches on the man's neck.

CHAPTER XIX.

In a room a woman sat at a table eating like a fat monk in a picture.

A soiled, unshaven man pushed open the door and entered.

"Well," said he, "Mag's dead."

"What?" said the woman, her mouth filled with bread.

"Mag's dead," repeated the man.

"Deh hell she is," said the woman. She continued her meal. When she finished her coffee she began to weep.

"I kin remember when her two feet was no bigger dan yer tumb, and she weared worsted boots," moaned she.

"Well, whata dat?" said the man.

"I kin remember when she weared worsted boots," she cried.

The neighbors began to gather in the hall,

staring in at the weeping woman as if watching the contortions of a dying dog. A dozen women entered and lamented with her. Under their busy hands the rooms took on that appalling appearance of neatness and order with which death is greeted.

Suddenly the door opened and a woman in a black gown rushed in with outstretched arms. "Ah, poor Mary," she cried, and tenderly embraced the moaning one.

"Ah, what ter'ble affliction is dis,'' continued she. Her vocabulary was derived from mission churches. "Me poor Mary, how I feel fer yehs! Ah, what a ter'ble affliction is a disobed'ent chile."

Her good, motherly face was wet with tears. She trembled in eagerness to express her sympathy. The mourner sat with bowed head, rocking her body heavily to and fro, and crying out in a high, strained voice that sounded like a dirge on some forlorn pipe.

"I kin remember when she weared worsted

boots an' her two feets was no bigger dan yer tumb an' she weared worsted boots, Miss Smith," she cried, raising her streaming eyes.

" Ah, me poor Mary," sobbed the woman in black. With low, coddling cries, she sank on her knees by the mourner's chair, and put her arms about her. The other women began to groan in different keys.

"Yer poor misguided chil' is gone now, Mary, an' let us hope its fer deh bes'. Yeh'll fergive her now, Mary, won't yehs, dear, all her dis-obed'ence ? All her tankless behavior to her mudder an' all her badness ? She's gone where her ter'ble sins will be judged."

The woman in black raised her face and paused. The inevitable sunlight came stream-ing in at the windows and shed a ghastly cheerfulness upon the faded hues of the room. Two or three of the spectators were sniffling, and one was loudly weeping. The mourner arose and staggered into the other room. In a moment she emerged with a pair of faded

Crane creates a semi-animal world

baby shoes held in the hollow of her hand.

"I kin remember when she used to wear dem," cried she.   The women burst anew into cries as if they had all been stabbed.   The mourner turned to the soiled and unshaven man.

"Jimmie, boy, go git yer sister! Go git yer sister an' we'll put deh boots on her feets!"

"Dey won't fit her now, yeh damn fool," said the man.

"Go git yer sister, Jimmie," shrieked the woman, confronting him fiercely.

The man swore sullenly.   He went over to a corner and slowly began to put on his coat. He took his hat and went out, with a dragging, reluctant step.

The woman in black came forward and again besought the mourner.

"Yeh'll fergive her, Mary! Yeh'll fergive yer bad, bad chil'! Her life was a curse an' her days were black an' yeh'll fergive yer

bad girl?   She's gone where her sins will be
judged."

"She's gone where her sins will be judged,"
cried the other women, like a choir at a
funeral.

"Deh Lord gives and deh Lord takes
away," said the woman in black, raising her
eyes to the sunbeams.

"Deh Lord gives and deh Lord takes away,"
responded the others.

"Yeh'll fergive her, Mary!" pleaded the
woman in black.   The mourner essayed to
speak but her voice gave way.   She shook her
great shoulders frantically, in an agony of
grief.   Hot tears seemed to scald her quivering
face.   Finally her voice came and arose like a
scream of pain.

"Oh, yes, I'll fergive her!   I'll fergive her!"